A Bandit's Betrayed Heart

A Blood Blade Sisters Novel

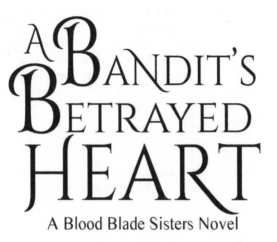

A Bandit's Betrayed Heart

A Blood Blade Sisters Novel

Michelle McLean

Entangled Publishing, LLC
10940 S Parker Rd
Suite 327
Parker, CO 80134
rights@entangledpublishing.com

Scandalous is an imprint of Entangled Publishing, LLC.

Edited by Erin Molta
Cover design by Erin Dameron-Hill

Manufactured in the United States of America

First Edition January 2014

To TCR - thank you for putting the smiles on my face. Love you always.

Chapter One

Seven years earlier

Lucy Richardson crept down the hallway, pausing every few feet to make sure the house remained still and quiet. If she were caught, there'd be hell to pay. She came to a stop in front of Finn's door, took one last look over her shoulder, and turned the knob. She held her breath until the door clicked open. He hadn't locked it. Lucy smiled and eased into his room.

She couldn't see anything except the faint glow of moonlight filtering in through a crack in the curtains. But it was enough to see Finn's form in the bed. She couldn't hear him breathing though and couldn't tell if he was asleep or awake.

"What are you doing, Lucy?"

Awake. She reached behind her and locked the door.

"Lucy," he said, his voice low, warning. "You shouldn't be here."

"I know," she whispered.

There were a million reasons she shouldn't be there. She and Finn weren't married and were not even courting. They couldn't get married, not without the biggest brouhaha Boston society had seen in a decade. Finn was not only her sister's butler, he had a murky past and a face covered in Mohave tribal tattoos. Lucy, on the other hand, was now one of the richest women in Boston thanks to a little gold mine on her family's ranch in California. For Finn and Lucy to marry would go against everything society dictated, but for them to be together without marriage was unthinkable.

But Lucy didn't care. She loved Finn. The very thought of him made her heart flutter and her breath catch. A brush of his hand made her skin tingle. And his kisses…well, his kisses obviously had the power to make her go stark, raving mad since she was creeping into the servants' quarters in the middle of the night for just one more taste of him.

"This is a bad idea, Lucy."

"I don't care," she said, climbing on the bed.

Despite his words, he wasn't making any move to evict her from his room. She reached out a tentative hand and found him. Her fingers tightened in the nightshirt straining over his chest. She pulled herself closer to him, let her hand trail up his chest to where the shirt opened. When her fingers brushed across his bare skin, he sucked in a breath.

She inched closer still, drew her hand up his neck to slip into his hair. With a groan, he wrapped her in his arms, crushing her to him as his lips descended. Lucy plastered herself to him, reveling in the hard planes of his body pressing against her soft curves. They'd stolen many a kiss in darkened corners, but this was the first time there had been so little clothing between them. The thin material of her nightdress and his shirt felt like nothing at all, but it was still too much. She longed for the heat of his bare skin against hers.

She reached down to grasp his hip, disappointed to find

that he still wore his breeches. He lifted his head when she paused, and she could see the white flash of his teeth in the moonlight.

"I thought you might wander into my room tonight."

"Well, don't you think you are a little overdressed for the occasion?"

He leaned down and kissed her again, letting his lips trail across her cheek to the sensitive skin under her ear.

"No. I think it's going to be the only hope I've got to keep from ravishing you."

"If I didn't want to be ravished, I wouldn't have come."

Finn chuckled. "Ah, darlin'. I'd love to oblige you."

Lucy made a little purring noise in the back of her throat that surprised even her and arched into him. Finn hissed and rolled her beneath him, his lips and hands creating a torrent of sensation that was almost too intense to bear.

"Finn," she whimpered, her hand straying down to the waistband of his pants.

"No," he said, catching her hand and entwining his fingers with hers.

"Why?" she whispered.

Finn dragged in a ragged breath and leaned his forehead against hers. With his body still pressed to hers, she could tell he was as affected as she was. So why was he hesitating?

"Lucy, you know things in my life are…complicated right now. There are things in my past that need to be dealt with before I can have any kind of a future with you."

"I know that, but…"

"No," he said again, leaning down to kiss her. "Do you have any idea how much I love you?"

Lucy grinned shyly. He'd told her he loved her, on more than one occasion, but her heart soared every time she heard those words on his lips.

"Finn…"

He brought their entwined hands up to his lips and kissed each of her fingers. "I want nothing more than to spend the rest of my life showing you exactly how much I love you. But until I get out of this mess that I'm in, I'm not free to build a life with you. I just need a little time."

"And if your grand plan to put your past to rights doesn't work out, what then?"

Finn sighed. "That's exactly the reason I'm not going to take advantage of you now."

"You aren't taking advantage of me, Finn."

Finn just shook his head. "I don't want to do something we can't undo. I won't risk leaving you alone with the consequences of our actions. I love you too much to drag you into my world. Someday, hopefully soon, I'll be free to live with you in peace. When that day comes, it will be the happiest I've ever known. But until then, we need to be careful."

Lucy ducked her head against his chest, shifting restlessly against him. "I know you think you're protecting me. But I don't care. I want you. So much it hurts to breathe."

"I know, love," he said, kissing her gently. "I know."

Lucy thought he'd pull back but to her delight, he didn't. His mouth explored hers until her head swam. His hand slipped inside her nightgown and Lucy froze.

"I thought you said…"

"I did. And I meant it. But that doesn't mean we can't do other things."

Before Lucy could ask what other things he meant, Finn set about showing her.

• • •

Finn kissed Lucy good-bye, letting his lips linger against hers. Sending her away was a near physical pain, but she couldn't be found in his room. From the moment he'd set eyes on her, all he'd wanted to do was protect her, from everything and everyone. Even himself, if necessary. Lucy was everything that was sweet and good in his life, though she had a backbone of steel and enough gumption to rule the world if she wished. She already ruled him. But she also had an unhealthy appetite for danger and a penchant for finding it.

Finn smiled and shook his head. When he'd come to Boston, he'd never expected anything like her. Never thought a woman could affect him so. Never thought he could love anyone so deeply.

He shied away from the thought. Finn had only ever loved one woman in his life before meeting Lucy. Rachel. And because of him...no, he refused to think of it. He didn't deserve happiness. Didn't deserve to love someone like Lucy, let alone have her love him in return.

But if the fates were merciful, perhaps he could prove himself worthy one day.

He watched her until she disappeared around the corner, the faint light from the early morning sun striking her hair and making the copper-colored tresses shimmer like a new penny. Finn closed his door and sank down on the edge of his bed, rubbing his burning eyes. The night he'd just spent loving Lucy had been the best night of his life. One he'd treasure always. No matter what happened. But it was going to make getting through the coming day extremely hard. For a variety of reasons. Finn shifted uncomfortably on the bed and finally flopped back onto his pillows.

What he wouldn't give to be able to march up to Lucy's sister and declare his love. Brynne wasn't Boston born and bred. She'd started life a poor rancher's daughter. He didn't think she'd be prejudiced against them.

But Brynne was the least of his worries. His employer— his other employer—could never find out about Lucy. If he knew Finn loved her, she'd just become collateral that could be used against him. Finn wouldn't put her in danger that way. He had to protect her at all costs. She couldn't end up like... like...Rachel.

The image of the last time he'd seen his first love flashed in his mind. Her broken and bloodied body tangled at his feet.

His heart clenched, and he sucked in a deep breath, trying to breathe through the pain that always struck him at Rachel's memory. The thought of anything happening to Lucy was unbearable. He'd sacrifice everything to keep her safe. Which meant, for the moment, that he needed to stay away from her. He didn't like the plan that was brewing between his partners, and until he found a way to get out from under his boss's thumb, Lucy's association with him put her in danger.

Finn was determined to find a way. A way to get free. And then he and Lucy could be together.

If he couldn't... Finn swallowed, the thought of leaving and never seeing Lucy's smiling face or looking into her deep brown eyes again striking him like a knife to the heart. There was no help for it though. If he couldn't escape the servitude he was under, he'd have to disappear. There was no other way to ensure Lucy's safety. His boss wouldn't hesitate to hurt her in order to get what he wanted from Finn. And Finn would die before he'd let that happen.

Hopefully, it wouldn't come to that. Because leaving her would be a fate worse than death.

Chapter Two

Seven years later

Lucy dipped her needle into her patient's hand one more time, slowly drawing the thread through until the last bit of the wound had closed. She deftly tied the thread off and snipped it with her little scissors. The man sitting before her let out a breath.

"All done," Lucy said, patting his hand. "Let me just wrap this up, and then you can be on your way."

"Thank you, miss. That didn't hardly hurt at all."

"I told you it wouldn't be as bad as you feared," she said with a wink. "I'm even better at stitching than my sister. But don't you tell her I said so."

"I heard that," Brynne said, depositing a fresh stack of bandages on the bedside table.

The man chuckled and looked back and forth between the sisters. "Doc Oliver is sure lucky having the two of you to help him out. Why, it's almost worth getting hurt just to be able to visit with the both of you."

Lucy finished bandaging his palm and gave his other hand a squeeze. "Mr. Eddings, you are welcome to visit any time you'd like, though we'd much prefer a visit when you aren't sporting a gaping wound." She smiled, helping the sweet old man to his feet. "Now, you be careful, you hear. I think you've had your limit of injuries for the month."

Mr. Eddings wheezed out a laugh and went to settle his account with Mrs. Birch, the clinic's formidable housekeeper.

Brynne stayed to help Lucy tidy up the exam area, and Lucy braced herself for the lecture she knew was coming.

"Richard ran into David Burrows this morning."

"Did he?" Lucy said, feigning ignorance. Brynne and her husband Richard had been arranging little meetings and outings with single men for years now, but lately their matchmaking efforts had risen to heights that would terrify a mountain goat. They just didn't seem to grasp that Lucy had no interest in marrying. Anyone. Ever.

"Oh, don't you go playing the innocent with me, Lucy Richardson. You know very well you left that boy twiddling his thumbs all night waiting for you!"

"I most certainly did not! I showed up. I just left a little early, that's all."

Brynne snorted. "You pretended to have a headache and left five minutes after arriving. You didn't even give poor David a chance. He's a perfectly nice young man. Handsome, from a good family. I swear, you'd find fault with a saint."

Lucy sighed. "There wasn't anything wrong with him. He seemed perfectly nice. He's just not…"

Brynne's eyes narrowed, and Lucy swallowed the name she'd almost let slip out. The name she'd promised herself over and over she'd never say again. He just wasn't…Finn.

Brynne's face softened as she gazed at her sister. She put down the linens she'd been folding and gathered Lucy in her arms, giving her a quick hug. Then she pulled back and looked

Lucy in the eyes, cupping Lucy's face in her hands. "You have to let him go, Lucy. It's been seven years. He's never coming back."

Lucy swallowed past the sudden lump in her throat. "I know. I'm trying." She stepped back, out of Brynne's embrace. "It's just that…"

Brynne sat down on the cot and patted the spot beside her. Lucy sat reluctantly. She really didn't want to have this conversation again.

"Lucy, believe me, I know what you are going through. After Jake died, I didn't think I'd ever fall in love again. I compared every man I met to Jake, and none of them ever came close to measuring up. But then I met Richard."

Brynne glanced around the clinic until she spotted her husband, deep in conversation with one of his patients on the far side of the clinic. "Even then, I almost let the memory of Jake ruin my chance for happiness."

Lucy opened her mouth to speak but Brynne continued on.

"I know you loved Finn," she said, her mouth hardening a bit as it always did when Finn was mentioned. She said she'd forgiven him for his role in her daughter's kidnapping all those years ago. But no matter what she said, Lucy knew she'd never forget it. Even if she understood his motives and no longer blamed him for what had happened.

"But," she pressed on, "you were so young. You didn't have a chance to have a real relationship with him and you are letting the memory of your first romance, such as it was, ruin your future."

Lucy stiffened, offended at the implication that what she felt for Finn was somehow lessened by the brevity of their relationship. "That is hardly fair, Brynne, especially coming from you. You married Jake when you'd hardly known each other and you were married a scant month before he died.

How long did you pine for him?"

Brynne's eyes narrowed. "That's different and you know it."

"How? How is it different? Because we didn't have the time to get married? Neither did you, if you want to point at specifics. You didn't even wait long enough for a proper wedding. You had Finn marry you, for crying out loud. It wasn't even legal. So don't dismiss how I feel, felt, for Finn because you are the last person who has the right to do so. I experienced more heart-pounding, soul-altering passion during my short time with Finn than I ever have with any of the men I've met since and frankly, I don't think it's possible to feel that again. We might not have had long together, but we loved a lifetime's worth. So don't you dare belittle it."

Brynne sat back. But after a moment she nodded and took Lucy's hand. "You're right. I was dismissing how you feel and, I, of all people, should know that the amount of time someone spends with a loved one cannot dictate the intensity of the love. But I can't bear to see you so unhappy. I don't doubt that you loved him, but it was a very long time ago, Lucy. Even I moved on, eventually. I'll always love Jake, but I've found happiness with Richard. There's so much love and passion and fulfillment that you haven't experienced yet. That's all I want for you."

Lucy looked down, not wanting to meet her sister's gaze. Brynne didn't know everything she and Finn had shared. She didn't know of the stolen kisses in hidden corners, all the moments spent whispering, planning, dreaming. Or of the night that Lucy had crept into Finn's room, into his bed, and had offered herself to him.

Lucy turned her head to hide the blush that still threatened to rise, all these years later, at the memory of that night. Brynne was wrong if she thought Lucy had never experienced passion. Finn had refused to take her innocence.

He'd insisted that they wait until they were properly wed. But they'd done other things. He'd spent the night showing her how he loved her in more ways than she could have ever imagined. They'd pledged themselves to each other.

And then...everything had gone to hell. And he'd been forced to run. She'd told him to run, told him to save himself. But she never dreamed that he wouldn't return for her.

"He is gone," Brynne said gently. "He left you standing there in that field. If he was going to come back for you, he'd have done so by now. And with the war...well, you can't be sure that he—"

"No," said Lucy, raising her hand for Brynne to stop. "Don't say it."

Lucy knew the chances were very good that Finn was dead. So many men had lost their lives during the war. So many would never be coming home. But Lucy refused to believe that Finn was one of them. She'd poured over the casualty sheets that had come in. His name had never been listed. But then, she had no idea where he'd been. Or even what side he'd been fighting for. For all she knew, he might have been fighting for the South. Or he might have gone to Europe to escape the conflict. Or perhaps he'd gone back to California and made amends with the Mohave tribe who'd raised him.

Brynne was right. Dead or alive, Finn was never coming back. He'd gone back on all his promises, chosen to leave her, and he'd made damn sure she'd never find him. So why couldn't she let him go? Find another man who could make her happy, who she could share her life with, have children with, grow old with?

She'd tried. She really had. But no one ever measured up. And she'd rather grow old alone, the spinster aunt to her sisters' children, than live in a joyless marriage just for the sake of being married.

Brynne watched Lucy for a moment and then gave her a quick one-armed hug. "All right, I'll let it drop for now."

Lucy rose gratefully and went about her work, hoping her sister had forgotten…

"Wait a minute."

No such luck.

"If you left David minutes after arriving at the theater, where were you all night? You didn't come home until well after midnight."

"I…went for a ride in the park."

Brynne's gaze darted around, and she leaned in closer so only Lucy would hear her hiss, "Lucy! You didn't."

Lucy put on her most innocent expression. With the war a year behind them, life was returning to normal, but there were still those who needed help. Those the sisters could assist in secret, leaving small gifts of goods or money when no one was looking. Brynne didn't mind Lucy riding off on those missions. She even helped as often as she could. But during the war, when times were hard and many were suffering, Lucy had found occasion to resurrect her old bandit persona in order to mete out a different sort of help. Brynne did not approve of Lucy's vigilante-style of justice. Lucy was always careful, but she was never one to turn away from a person in need. And if that meant trussing up a few bad characters before they could get away with their crimes, then Lucy didn't see the harm in it.

Brynne, however, disagreed. But Brynne had done more than that in her day, so she could hardly protest too much, and Lucy heartily needed something to bring a little excitement into her life. She was happy working in her brother-in-law's clinic and helping to look after her nieces and nephews. But a girl had to do something to get her blood pumping every now and then.

"Lucy!" Brynne hissed again.

"I was careful. Don't worry."

Before Brynne could really get into her browbeating, Mrs. Birch escorted another patient into the exam area. Lucy took the opportunity to escape her sister and rushed to help the man to a cot.

"This isn't over," Brynne whispered to her as Lucy got the man settled. "We'll discuss it at home."

Lucy smiled over her shoulder at Brynne, ignoring her sister's glare, and turned her attention to the man before her.

"Hi, there," she said, smiling. "What can we do for you today?"

"Well, ma'am, I fell crossing the road yesterday. Landed on my arm hard. It always acts up a bit now and then, since the war."

Lucy nodded her head sympathetically as she rolled up his sleeve, exposing a tangled mass of scars running up the length of his arm.

"You were lucky you were able to keep the arm," she said, awe in her voice.

"Yes, ma'am, that's the right honest truth. Thought for sure the doctor was going to amputate a few times, but we hung in there." He patted his arm with a laugh. "Still aches like the dickens sometimes, especially when it's cold or there's a storm coming. And it seems to be a bit weaker than the other one. Can't grasp things near as well, that sort of thing."

Lucy nodded and continued her examination while he spoke. She'd definitely have Richard come look at it, though she was pretty sure she knew the problem. Still, she was only a nurse, not a doctor, and not even a properly trained one at that. When the war hit, Richard had expanded his clinic, taking in as many wounded as he could. Brynne and Lucy had gotten a crash course in nursing, though Brynne had already been helping in the clinic. By the time the war ended, they were both fair nurses.

Lucy helped full time most days, though Brynne didn't spend as much time in the clinic as she used to. Coraline was almost in her teens and becoming quite a handful, and her younger brother and sister were keeping Brynne very busy. With the war over and the demands on Brynne's attention lessened, she was spending as much time as she could with her children.

"Well, Mr...."

"Watley."

"Mr. Watley, I'm fairly certain you've sprained your arm. I'll have the doctor come take a look to be certain. But as far as I can tell, you haven't broken it."

"Well, that's a blessing, miss."

Lucy smiled kindly at him and looked up to catch Richard's eye. He nodded and held up a finger, indicating he'd be a minute.

Lucy settled into the chair by the cot. "Where were you when you were injured?"

"You'll have to be more specific, miss," Mr. Watley said with a laugh.

"Your arm." Lucy laughed along with him. It felt good to laugh again. And she was glad Mr. Watley could have a good sense of humor about it. A rare gift under the current circumstances, for certain.

"Ah, my poor arm. Well that one happened in the Battle of Cedar Creek. Cannon blast hit the wagon I was hiding behind. Blew it to bits. Most of which ended up in my arm."

"Oh, I'm so sorry. How awful."

"Not at all, miss," he said with a huge grin. "This arm," he patted it fondly, "saved my poor face from taking the full brunt. Only one little sliver caught me, just here." He turned his head to show her a thin, jagged scar running up his jaw line to his ear. "Yes, ma'am, I've got a good arm here, that's for certain."

Lucy smiled, amused at the man's fondness for his arm. He spoke of it as if it were a beloved pet. And she applauded his ability to find a way to be happy over his troubles.

"Well, we'll have to make sure we take good care of that arm then. You were lucky indeed to have it with you that day."

"Oh yes, ma'am, that's for certain. Even more lucky that I had Fish with me."

"Fish?" Lucy said, almost afraid to ask. "You had a lucky fish with you?"

"Ha!" Mr. Watley chortled so hard his face turned bright red. "Ah, bless you, miss. Not a real fish. A man."

"A man named Fish?"

Mr. Watley was still chuckling. "Well, that's what we all called him. A right good soldier he was. Fearless. Always running off on crazy missions. Like he had a death wish or something. Only nothing ever touched him. Oh, he was wounded a time or two. I don't think a man alive escaped without some sort of damage or another. But nothing ever bad enough to slow him down. Not Fish. Never seen a man like him. Saved my life more than once. And my ugly mug a time or two as well."

Lucy smiled and patted Mr. Watley's hand. "You were lucky indeed to have him."

Richard came over and introduced himself, quickly getting to work wrapping the arm that was, as Lucy had suspected, sprained.

Lucy kept up her conversation with Mr. Watley to help distract him from any discomfort he might be feeling.

"Why did you call your friend Fish, Mr. Watley?"

"Oh, well, because that's what he looked like."

Lucy grinned. "He looked like a fish? How so?"

"Oh, you'd never seen a man like him before, miss, I can promise you that. He'd probably frighten the wits out of a gentle thing like you. Used to fair scare them graybacks when he'd go runnin' at them, all fierce and furious. You've never seen a thing like it."

"Well, a fierce warrior doesn't sound much like a fish to me," Lucy said, helping Mr. Watley to stand once Richard had finished with his arm.

Mr. Watley chuckled again. "It was them lines he had on his face."

Lucy stopped short. The blood rushed from her face, leaving it ice cold and frozen. She could see Mr. Watley looking at her with concern but couldn't force a reassuring smile to save her life. Her head felt curiously light, as if it would float off at any second. But her heart pounded so hard it hurt, each beat a painful stab to her chest.

"He had lines on his face?" she heard herself ask, though she had no conscious thought to speak.

"Yes, miss. Here now, are you all right? Doctor!"

"Lines...marks...two T-shaped marks just here?" she asked, pointing to her cheekbones.

"That's right, miss. How did you know?"

"And more lines...five lines, going from his lower lip to his chin?"

"Yes, miss. Always looked a bit like fish gills, I thought. And then with his name...Fish just fit."

"His name? A fish name?"

"What is it?" Richard asked, having come at a run at Mr. Watley's call. "Lucy, what's wrong?"

Richard grasped her arm, bending over her, his eyes round with concern. She pushed him aside so she could see Mr. Watley again.

"A fish name?" she asked again, her voice sounding shrill and desperate even to her own ears.

"Yes, miss. Finn his name was. Well, that wasn't his real name, just the short version. His real name was—"

"Finnegan," Lucy whispered, black spots beginning to

lick at the corners of her vision.

"Yes, miss. That's it." Mr. Watley was astounded. "Finnegan Taggart."

Lucy barely registered the sight of Richard jumping forward to catch her before her vision went completely black and she was sucked into blessed nothingness.

Chapter Three

Lucy grabbed another petticoat and shoved it in her trunk. Brynne stood in the doorway, her year-old son James on her hip. Lucy determinedly kept from meeting Brynne's eyes. She didn't want to see her sister's thin-lipped disapproval. Or the fear in her eyes that she was trying so hard not to show.

Her brother-in-law Richard came to stand behind his wife and son. He put a hand on Brynne's shoulder. "You have nothing to worry about, Brynne."

Brynne snorted. "I wouldn't say 'nothing.' My head-cracked sister might just be the death of me yet."

Richard chuckled and Lucy turned her head so her sister wouldn't see her smile.

"It's not funny, Richard! She's going all alone. She might get hurt or get in trouble or—"

Richard laughed again, ignoring Brynne's glare. "She's a Richardson, Brynne. She rode the trails with you and robbed stagecoaches when she was barely old enough to sit a horse, for heaven's sake. I'm more worried about the poor citizens of whatever city she's going to tear apart to find that man."

"Thank you, Richard," Lucy said, rolling her eyes at him.

Brynne's lip twitched, amusement breaking through the worry on her face. Richard took James from her and kissed her on the forehead. "We'll just wait downstairs."

Lucy gave her brother-in-law a grateful smile. He winked at her and then left, leaving her alone with Brynne.

Lucy turned to her sister. "Look. I know you worry about me. But I'm more than capable of taking care of myself. You and Cilla were in your teens when Mama and Papa died. But I was just a little girl. Hell, I grew up riding the trails with you, fighting off Frank and his goons to keep the ranch and the town afloat. I was able to shoot a tick off a dead dog's back before I was old enough to put my hair up."

Brynne sighed. "I know. You're as tough as they come, no doubt about it. But that doesn't mean I don't worry about you. I don't care how old you get or how strong and tough you are. You're always going to be my baby sister. And I hate that you are going to do this alone. If you'd just wait…or let one of us go with you."

"You have children to care for. You don't need to be dragging them all over the South. And I'm not going to take Richard away from his patients, though I know he would willingly come if I asked. I will be fine on my own. In fact, I prefer to go alone. If I need you, you're just a telegram away."

"I know. It's just…"

Lucy closed the lid of the trunk and leaned on it for a moment, closing her eyes while she concentrated on reining in the overwhelming panic that had been gnawing at her since Mr. Watley's revelation. She had never been so excited, or so terrified, in her life. There were so many what-ifs running rampant through her mind that her temples pounded with the force of them.

What if Mr. Watley had been mistaken? What if she couldn't find him? The thought of what would happen and how she'd feel, if the hope building in her chest was crushed once again was staggering. She'd barely survived losing him the first time. She didn't think she could do it again.

And that was the crux of the dilemma, wasn't it? What if she did find him and he didn't want her? Didn't love her anymore, or worse, didn't even remember her? Wouldn't it be better to leave things as they were? At least now she had her good memories to hold onto. If she looked for him, things could end so much worse.

Then again, what if she found him and all her dreams came true?

But how often did that happen?

Lucy raised a shaking hand to her stomach and closed her eyes. Her mind, body, and soul were in turmoil. Once she started on this journey, there was no going back. She'd found a sort of peace in the life she had. Was it worth it to risk that peace? When doing so might shatter her beyond repair?

"What would you do, Brynne?" Lucy whispered. "If someone told you'd they'd seen Jake...would you go? Just to see? Just to make sure?"

She finally looked up at her sister, knowing it was unfair to use her deceased brother-in-law against Brynne but wanting her to understand, to support her decision.

Brynne held her stony-faced expression for a second longer, and then her face fell. She came into the room and sat on the bed. "Yes," she said quietly. "I would go."

Lucy let a sob escape and sat beside her sister, welcoming Brynne's embrace. She let Brynne hold her and rock her, just as she had when they were children.

It had been seven long years since the night Finn had left. Running from the law, and from Brynne's wrath, after his part in the kidnapping of Coraline. He'd only done it to protect Coraline from his smuggling partners when they had decided to kidnap her for ransom in order to recoup their losses from

Brynne's bandit activities. But with his partners dead and the police bearing down on him, Finn had fled for his life.

Lucy understood. It had been necessary at the time. She'd wanted him to go, told him to flee to safety. But she hadn't thought he'd stay away forever. Eventually Brynne had calmed down and had come to understand that he'd only done what he needed to in order to protect her daughter. The police were no longer looking for him. But still he hadn't returned. Lucy had heard nothing from him except for a note he'd sent a month after he'd disappeared, letting her know he was all right. She'd gone to look for him. And hadn't found him.

Then the war started, and everyone's life had been thrown into chaos. But Lucy had thought of Finn every waking day.

"I still dream of him nearly every night," Lucy whispered. "But his face isn't clear anymore. Sometimes I'm afraid I'll forget it entirely. But when I dream, I hear his voice as if he's standing next to me."

"Oh, Lucy," Brynne said, hugging her sister tighter.

"I know you wish I'd marry one of the suitors you've found for me. Sometimes I wish I could. I wish I could fall in love with someone else, let go of Finn once and for all. But I can't. How can I pledge myself to another when nearly every night I hear *his* voice in my dreams? And then wake in the morning feeling his loss all over again." Lucy shook her head. "I'll never marry. I don't think I'm capable of loving anyone else." She laughed. "Besides, I'm already an old maid. Who would want me?"

Brynne sniffed. "Old maid. Hardly. Any man would be lucky to have you."

Lucy sat up and gave her a sad smile. "No. I can't burden a man with a wife who could never love him as he deserved."

"Lucy, you don't know that you can't love another. You've never really tried. You compare everyone you meet to Finn, and perhaps that is natural. But you've never truly and properly tried to let him go. You've always hung on to the hope that he'd come back someday. How can you move on with your future if you are still so tightly holding onto the past? I know this is hard to hear, but on this subject, I know what I'm talking about."

Lucy sighed. Brynne was right. Though she had tried to let Finn go. Truly. She filled her sleepless nights with secret charity drops and the occasional black-masked act of banditry or vigilante justice...anything she could do to keep her mind from dwelling too long on Finn. Nothing had worked.

But now...now she had news of him. He was alive! And she had a good chance of finding him. Mr. Watley had seen him just a month prior, down in Charlotte. He'd been happy to run into his old friend, though Finn had apparently not been as happy to see Mr. Watley. Mr. Watley chalked it up to the war. No one had come away unscathed and few wanted to be reminded of those days. From the stories Mr. Watley told her, Finn seemed to have tried his level best to get himself killed. All he'd succeeded in doing was to commit more heroic acts than anyone else in the regiment.

Now Lucy knew where he was. She only prayed he was still there.

Even greater than her fear that he would leave again was another fear. One that made her nauseous with dread.

"What if he doesn't remember me?" she whispered, hardly daring to give the fear voice.

Brynne scoffed. "Not possible."

"But it's been so long. I was hardly more than a child when he left."

Brynne gazed at her long and hard. Finally she grasped her hand. "You never forget the ones you love, Lucy. They burrow their way into your heart and never let go, no matter how many years may pass. Even if the love you once felt is no longer there, a piece of your heart will always belong to that other person.

"I'm not going to promise you that he still cares for you. It has been a long time, and much has happened to change you both since you've last seen one another. But I will promise you that he hasn't forgotten you. He loved you once. Even I could see that, though I didn't want to," Brynne said with a smile.

"I'm not going to pretend that I'm happy with you going to find him," she continued. "But I understand why you need to go. If you don't, you'll always wonder. Perhaps once you've seen him, once you've laid the ghosts of your past to rest, you'll be able to move on with your life. Move on and find some happiness. That's all I want for you. And I don't think you'll be able to truly let yourself be happy until you've made your peace with him."

Lucy hugged her sister. "Thank you," she whispered.

Brynne stood, quickly wiping at her eyes. "Well, you'd better hurry, or the train will be leaving without you."

Lucy gave her a watery smile and grabbed her coat and hat. Finally, she'd see him again.

Excitement and terror warred with each other in the pit of her stomach. Maybe this trip wasn't a good idea. But it wasn't a choice really. If he wasn't happy to see her...Well, she just prayed she'd be strong enough to walk away again. But at least she'd know for sure.

Chapter Four

Lucy turned the letter over and over in her hand. She'd read the brief note a thousand times, ten thousand times maybe, since it had been delivered. She'd kept it all through the war, looking at it whenever her loneliness had grown too overwhelming. The letter made her feel closer to him somehow. Reading it once more wouldn't reveal anything new. But she couldn't help herself.

I'm safe. Please don't look for me. Have a good life. Be happy.

Be happy. Certainly. Perhaps if she could cut out her heart and grow a new one, she'd be able to find happiness without him. She'd tried. For years, she'd tried. After he'd gone, she'd courted every young man her family had thrown at her. She gone to parties and socials, she'd filled countless dance cards and accepted invitation after invitation. But every man she met had paled in comparison to Finn.

During the war, she had volunteered her services in the clinic, working beside Brynne and Richard until she'd dropped into bed each night, so weary she couldn't dream.

Since the war, she'd thrown herself into her work even more. Anything to keep busy, to keep her mind from straying to the love she'd lost. But nothing kept her visions of Finn at bay. His face haunted her waking hours and tormented her dreams. She had to find him, if only to lay the ghost to rest. Whether or not he remembered her, let alone wanted her still. But either way, she hoped finding him, seeing him again, would allow her in some way to move on.

"Charlotte, next stop!" the conductor announced.

Lucy gathered her shawl and slipped it over her shoulders. She had little hope that Finn was still in Charlotte, where Mr. Watley had seen him several weeks ago. But there was nothing to do but follow his trail. Surely, once she was here she'd hear some word of him. A man with Mohave tribal markings tattooed on his face would be hard to miss.

She stood and waited by the door to her first-class cabin for the train to come to a stop. The train slowed and Lucy exited the minute it jerked to a halt. She stood for a brief moment on the platform, unprepared for the heat that slapped her in the face. It was like trying to breathe through a wet blanket. She pulled off her shawl and made a mental note to schedule in some time to shop for some lighter clothing. Summers in Boston were hot, but the humidity in the South was something she'd never experienced before.

Lucy whipped out her fan, glad to have a little relief. But once the surprise of the heat dissipated, the enormity of her task overwhelmed her. People bustled all around her. How would she ever find him?

She only allowed herself a second to feel pity. For the first time in seven years she had word of him. Faint hope flickered through her. But that was more than she'd had in a long time. It was enough. She shook herself and looked at the letter in her hand. She might not know where he was right at that moment, but she knew where he'd been. Mr. Watley had seen

Finn at the Chatford Hotel. Might as well start there.

Lucy headed to the main road and hired a carriage to take her to the hotel. On the drive there, she focused on breathing slowly, in and out. She'd never been anywhere alone before, let alone in a strange city. But hell, once upon a time, she'd covered her face with a mask and played the bandit, risking the wrath of her corrupt half brother to deliver much needed money and supplies to the besieged people of her town. Being the new girl shouldn't be too hard.

The carriage pulled up to the Chatford Hotel and Lucy descended and marched right up to the desk, which was blessedly free from customers. The man behind the counter gave her a polite smile.

"Good afternoon, miss. How may I help you?"

"I need a room please."

"Certainly. Are you checking in alone?" The man glanced behind her, his brow creased.

"Oh no, of course not. My husband has business in town and sent me along to get things ready for us here."

"Ah, of course, of course," he said, his face clearing. "Well then. Just sign the register here, please," he said, indicating the next blank line in his book.

Lucy took the proffered pen and signed Mr. and Mrs. Finnegan Taggart.

She wasn't sure what possessed her to use Finn's name. She should have used something more common. Mr. and Mrs. Jones perhaps. But the sight of *Mrs. Taggart* sent a thrill rushing through her that was hard to contain.

Lucy didn't like lying and under normal circumstances wouldn't care if people knew she was traveling alone, but she had realized as she traveled South that people gave her less of a hassle if they assumed she was married. If they thought she had someone to look after her, they were less inclined to try and do so themselves. The last thing she needed was an overly helpful and concerned hotel clerk hounding her every move, trying to protect her. Besides, if she found Finn, it would make matters much easier if a man was seen going into her room.

That thought sent warmth spreading to long-forgotten parts of her and Lucy fought to keep a blank face. But she was a realist. She loved him and she'd been pining for him for seven very long years. If she were to find him again and discover that he'd been missing her as much as she'd been missing him…well, a disapproving desk clerk wasn't going to stop her from hauling Finn into her room and locking the door behind them.

The clerk took the pen back from her and turned the book back toward him. "Well now, we live in a small world, to be sure."

"Pardon?"

"We have another Finnegan Taggart staying at the hotel. I wonder if he could be kin to your man."

It took Lucy a second to respond. Her face felt as if it was frozen in ice but she forced a smile. "It could be. I suppose there are a number of Finnegan Taggarts running about."

The clerk chuckled. "I'm sure you're right. Well, now, here is your key. You are in room number 325. I'll just have the porter bring your bags up." He snapped his fingers and a boy ran up with an eager grin and grasped the handles of her bags.

"Will there be anything else?" the clerk asked when Lucy hesitated by the desk.

She had to ask. The coincidence was too much. "Yes. Actually, this might sound a bit odd, but I was wondering, have you seen anyone unusual perhaps? He might have some…markings on his face?"

Lucy didn't want to describe Finn in too much detail in case he was traveling in disguise. It hadn't occurred to her to ask Mr. Watley if Finn's tattoos had been covered when he'd seen him, and he hadn't mentioned it. She had no idea what he'd been doing for the last several years, but based on his past business partners…well, she was sure there were people he'd rather not run into. Asking about a man with facial tattoos would be as memorable as seeing the tattoos themselves, or nearly so. No point in making this conversation any more memorable than necessary, for both Finn's and her sake.

"No, Mrs. Taggart, I'm sorry. No one like that."

"Well, he's tall, blue eyes, light red hair…"

The clerk broke into a huge smile. "Now, that I can help with. The other Mr. Taggart I mentioned…"

"Yes?" Lucy whispered, her blood roaring in her ears.

"He fits that description."

"Do you…?" Lucy forced herself to breathe and slow down, though it took all her willpower not to jump over the desk and shake the clerk by the lapels until he spilled every last drop of information he had about Finn. "Do you perhaps know where I can find him?"

"Certainly, ma'am. He's right there."

"What?"

The clerk jumped at her shrill voice. "There, ma'am." The clerk pointed to the bustling lobby behind her.

Lucy turned, her heart dancing in her chest. She gripped her room key so tightly it bit into her flesh.

"Thank you," she managed to choke out.

The clerk looked at her, a confused frown furrowing his brow, but his attention was thankfully taken by another guest.

Lucy stared in the direction the clerk had pointed, her vision going blurry at the edges. She took a deep breath, forcing herself to rein in her rioting emotions.

Finn looked different without his tattoos visible, but it was definitely him crossing the hotel lobby. He was older. His handsome face looked weary with a sharpness to it that hadn't been there before. It took everything Lucy had to keep from running to him right there and then. But she didn't want their reunion played out in the middle of a hotel lobby. What if he didn't want to see her? What if...what if he was there with someone else? What if he was married? Lucy swallowed down the nausea that rose at that thought.

Tiny stabs of jealousy pricked at her with every pair of female eyes that Finn drew to him. Covering his tattoos was a smart move on his part, and it certainly helped him blend in, to a certain degree. But if he'd been hoping to avoid notice, he'd vastly misjudged his appeal. Six feet of muscled, strawberry-blond goodness with striking blue eyes were enough to make any woman forget her name.

Lucy missed the tattoos though. They were so much a part of him that he didn't seem complete without them.

Finn started up the stairs leading to the guest rooms. Lucy strode to the staircase. The key to blending in, she'd often found, was to act as if you were supposed to be there. While she had every right to be in the hotel, following a man up to his room was not something a decent woman would do. As long as she didn't appear furtive about it, no one should suspect she wasn't where she was supposed to be. She kept her head up, her eyes ahead, and marched up the steps as if she knew where she was going. She only hoped Finn wouldn't notice he was being followed.

At the landing, she turned left and hoped she'd chosen the right direction. She gasped and whirled around. Finn's retreating back was entering a room several doors down from where she stood. Lucy pretended to fix her bonnet, fiddling with it and gazing at her reflection in one of the mirrors that dotted the hallway until she heard his door close. She cautiously glanced over her shoulder.

Seeing no one, Lucy hurried to the door she'd seen him enter, her heart nearly beating from her chest. She was about to see him again. Confront him about leaving. Find out where he'd been, what he'd been doing. Stare into those eyes again.

Touch him. Breathe him in.

By the time she reached his door, the anticipation building in her was damn near suffocating. What if he had a wife and children behind that door? What if he didn't remember her? The last time he'd seen her, she'd been a fresh-faced eighteen-year-old. Now she was twenty-five. A far cry from the young girl he'd fallen in love with.

She reached out to knock, then hesitated. What if he no longer loved her? It had been so long. Surely he'd moved on.

The flood of butterflies in her stomach rioted, her nerves overwhelming her. She should just leave well enough alone. She'd seen him. She'd seen that he was alive and well. Perhaps it was enough. If she walked away now, she'd at least be able to hold on to her fantasy awhile longer. Because if she knocked on that door only to be rejected or to find that he'd moved on...she didn't think she could bear it.

She took a step back and frowned. His door was slightly ajar. The Finn she knew would never be so careless. Before she could back away farther, the door flew open and Finn grabbed her arm and hauled her inside. The door slammed behind her and Lucy found herself pressed against the wall, Finn's large hand wrapped about her neck, not squeezing, but most definitely imprisoning her.

He locked the door, his eyes never leaving her. Lucy's lungs screamed. She couldn't draw in air fast enough. The initial rush of fear had melted into awareness. This was Finn. Her Finn. He held her captive, every inch of his body pressed against her, his gaze roving over her face as though he hadn't eaten for an eternity and she were the juiciest piece of meat on the table.

The anger faded from his face the longer he stared at her. His fingers relaxed as finally recognition dawned. "Lucy?"

"Finn," she whispered. But that was as far as she got.

He crushed his lips to hers, kissing her with a desperation

that all but broke her heart. He pulled her against him, molding their bodies together. Lucy flung her arms about him, pressing as close to him as she could. He felt the same. Tasted the same. For a moment, it was as though no time at all had passed. A small sob escaped her throat, a sound that conveyed both her euphoria at finally being in his arms, and her frustration that they had so many layers of clothing between them. She wanted to feel every inch of him, feel his skin against hers. Engrain his very essence into her own so that he could never leave her again.

He tore his lips from hers, cupped her face in his hands, staring as though he couldn't believe she was really there. She smiled, a laugh choking through her tears of joy. He was really there. In her arms again. Her heart was going to burst with happiness.

She reached up to tangle her hands in his hair, bring his lips back to hers, but he stopped her, grasping her wrists as he broke away from her. His eyes narrowed, his jaw clenched. She could see him shutting down, closing off from her.

"Finn?"

He spun away and Lucy's knees nearly buckled in despair.

"What are you doing here?" He kept his back to her, his head hanging, defeated.

"Looking for you."

"Why?" he asked, so quietly Lucy almost didn't hear him. He looked at her, those beautiful blue eyes burning into hers. "Why?" This time the word was harsh, anguished, ripped from his throat.

"I…I wanted to see you. Make sure you were okay. You left without a word and then there was the war and I didn't know…I've wondered, worried…"

Finn paced, liked some caged animal that was being goaded by malicious spectators. Lucy swallowed the lump in her throat, not wanting to acknowledge that her fantasies were crumbling around her.

"How did you find me?"

"Does it matter?"

Finn's gaze shot to hers and Lucy straightened. He was different, harsher somehow. But he was still her Finn. And she was a Richardson, damn it. She refused to be intimidated by anyone.

"You just wipe that glare right off your face, Finnegan Taggart. I've traveled all the way from Boston with my heart in my throat—praying for the chance to get to see you again, make sure all was well with you. Last time I saw you, you told me you loved me, and while you might not feel the same after all these years, I thought what we had was special enough that we deserved the chance to find out. So here I am. And if you aren't happy about me being here, well then, you can just say so and I'll be on my way. But there isn't any call for you to be glaring at me like I've done something wrong because the only one in the wrong here is *you*."

Finn stared for a moment, blinking a few times before his lips pulled into a reluctant smile. He shook his head and looked at the floor. "I'd almost forgotten what a corker you are, Lucy Richardson." He looked up at her. "Never met anyone with as much gumption as you. I'm glad you never lost that."

He held his hand out, pointing to an armchair near the window. "Sit?"

Lucy eyed him warily, but he seemed to have shelved the antagonism for the moment so she perched on the edge of the chair, watching him as he took a seat opposite her.

"You look well, Lucy. I'm glad to see that. How have you been?"

Lucy wasn't quite sure how to answer that question. Physically, she was fine. Perfect. But emotionally, she was a wreck and had been since the day Finn had walked away.

So she settled for a noncommittal, "Fine."

Finn's eyebrow quirked up and Lucy had to bite her lip to keep from smiling. Seven years or no, he still seemed to know her. Know when she was holding back.

"I'm fine. Really. I've been helping out in Richard's clinic since the war started."

Finn nodded. "I wondered how you fared. I'm glad to find you well."

"You could have found that out at any time. Why did you never return?"

"You know why."

"I know why you left. Or I know why you left Boston, in any case. Though I still think it was unnecessary. Brynne calmed down and saw reason eventually, just as I told you she would."

Finn snorted. "Really? I would have bet my last penny that she would still want to skin me alive."

"It took a while, but eventually she understood. She knows things would have been worse for Coraline if you hadn't taken her. We know you had no choice. And I suppose I understand why you felt you had to leave Boston, at the time. But I want to know why you left *me*. Why didn't you take me with you? Send for me? Or at the very least, let me know where you were? Let me know you were all right? Still alive? So many were lost in the war, and I never knew…never knew if you'd been lost, too."

Finn looked out the window, the ordeals of the last seven years etched into his handsome face. "I guess I didn't think it mattered anymore. I left. It was done with. Why dredge it back up?"

"Because I never stopped loving you," Lucy said, her words hardly more than a whisper.

Finn blanched, his eyes closing, shutting her out. Lucy held her breath, waiting for him to respond. Waiting for him to pull her into his arms again, tell her how much he loved her, how happy he was that she had found him.

"You don't know what love is," he murmured instead.

Lucy's breath rushed out of her and it took all she had not to cry aloud. But he wasn't finished yet.

"You are too young to understand what you are saying. What you felt for me was nothing more than an infatuation. It will pass. It probably has passed. You are just holding onto something that no longer exists."

Lucy's chest heaved as she sucked in one lungful of air after another, hoping the oxygen would calm the nausea rising in her belly. And with the anguish came anger. She stood.

"I'm not the little girl you left in Boston all those years ago. I'm not a child to be told how she feels and doesn't feel. How dare you try to belittle how I feel?"

"You might be older now, but you *were* little more than a child when we met. And much has happened since then. I'm not the same man you knew back then and you," he said, staring ardently at her despite his words, "have changed as well, I'm sure. The war halted everyone's lives in some way, I think. Whatever feelings you think you still have for me are just remnants of the past."

Lucy's hands curled into fists at her sides. She tried to rein in her mounting frustration but it was proving difficult.

Finn stood. "You might still have some lingering feelings for me because you haven't had the opportunity to find something real."

"Oh, bull's balls!"

Finn's mouth dropped open and he slowly blinked. Normally, Lucy would be mortified at her lapse into her former heathen slang, but the man was beyond endurance.

"I might have been young back then, but I wasn't stupid. Don't you dare try to tell me how I felt then, or how I feel now. I'm not a little girl, Finn. Don't try to treat me like one."

Finn watched her for a moment, as though he were sizing her up. And then he nodded. "You're right. You aren't a little girl. And you weren't back then either, not really. I don't think you've ever truly been young. You went straight from diapers to a bandit's mask and then into a bloody war. You've never been one of those immature, flighty girls who doesn't know her own mind. My apologies."

Lucy took a deep breath and nodded, accepting his apology. Some of the fight had seeped out of her. She hadn't been sure what to expect when she found Finn, but having to talk him into loving her wasn't something that had occurred to her. Either he still loved her or he didn't. It should be as simple as that. Best to find out and get it over with.

"Did you ever marry?" she asked. She held her breath, waiting for his answer.

"No. I never married."

Lucy's heart soared for one brief moment, until he spoke again. "There's never been anyone I wished to marry. There never will be."

If he had reached into her chest and ripped her heart out, it wouldn't have hurt more than those words did. The lump in her throat damn near strangled her but she refused to let him see how much he'd wounded her.

And still…she couldn't give up. There was something he was hiding from her. Something in his eyes when he looked at her.

"I told you not to look for me," he said. "I told you to leave me be. How did you find me?"

"A patient at the clinic told me about a tattooed soldier he'd fought with in the war. A man with a death wish who fought like the devil himself. Who they called Fish," she said with a faint smile. "Who else could he have meant, but you?"

"Watley?"

Lucy nodded.

"I should have left after he found me. I never dreamed he'd find you, too."

"Perhaps it's fate."

Finn's eyebrow cocked again. "Since when do you believe in fate?"

Lucy shrugged. "I'm not sure what I believe in anymore."

"Lucy," Finn whispered.

And there it was again. That tone in his voice. That look in his eye. *That's* why she couldn't just walk away from him. He did still love her. No matter what he said. Somewhere deep in that damaged heart of his, he cared for her. She *knew* it. Knew it, with every fiber of her rapidly fraying being.

She closed the distance between them and wrapped her arms about his waist. For half a heartbeat, he returned her embrace. And then he set her away from him.

"Go home, Lucy. I don't want you here."

"Then why did you kiss me?"

Finn's jaws clench. "You surprised me. I wasn't expecting to ever see you again and then you were there…"

Lucy made a minute move toward him again and he backed up. "It was a reflex, a mistake. One I won't be repeating. You shouldn't be here, Lucy."

"I know you love me, Finn. And I love you. That's why I'm here. Because I couldn't let the only man I've ever loved just disappear from my life. Why can't you just be truthful?"

"I have never been more truthful in my life than when I say that I do not want you here."

Lucy's vision blurred with tears she refused to let fall. Each word was like a wasp's sting piercing her heart. The words she'd meant to say melted away under the intensity of his gaze.

"Why are you doing this?"

He looked at her again, let her see into the depths of those deep blue eyes. She could drown in those eyes and would do so willingly if he'd let her. "You don't belong with me, Lucy. I'm no good for you. I'm no good for anyone."

Lucy opened her mouth to protest but Finn raised his hand. "No. This won't work. I told you this back in Boston. The years have changed nothing. Go home. Go find some handsome, respectable young man and forget about me. And let me forget about you."

Finn made to walk past her to the door, but stopped, his shoulders dropping. He half turned his face toward her and Lucy filled with hope that he'd changed his mind. That he'd declare he'd been mad to try and send her away. Then he stiffened, his body rigid with determination, and pinned her with a hard gaze.

"Wait a few minutes after I leave. Make sure no one sees you leaving my room. Neither of us needs the scandal."

To Lucy's everlasting shame, a sob escaped her throat and the tears that had been burning behind her eyes finally fell.

Finn's face softened and he closed the distance between them. He cupped his hand behind her neck, brushing his thumb across her cheek.

"Finn," she whispered.

He kissed her forehead, his lips brushing across her skin so faintly she could barely feel them.

"Go home, Lucy. I don't want you here."

And then he was gone.

Lucy stared at the closed door long after he left while she struggled to stifle the heartbreak that was crushing her soul. Finally, she started to pull herself together, one emotional thread at a time, until she was able to shove her roiling emotions deep down and square her shoulders with new resolve.

Finn might have said he didn't want her there, but he was lying. To her and to himself. And she was going to make damn sure she made him face the truth. He still loved her.

For the first time in many years, she felt a spark of her old fire. She had something to fight for again, and Richardsons never backed down from a fight.

Go home?

"No way in hell," she muttered.

Chapter Five

Finn strode down the hallway and back down the grand staircase of the hotel, hardly seeing where he was going. He couldn't believe she was really there. When he'd first seen her, he'd half thought she was a dream. What was she doing here?

He shouldn't have kissed her. That had been a mistake. He could still taste her on his lips. Still feel her pressed against him. He could never let that happen again. It would do nothing more than hurt her further and wound him past the point of endurance. How many times had he wished he could hold her in his arms just one more time? Well, he'd gotten his wish. And now the memory of that kiss would be a bittersweet torture for the rest of his miserable life.

The pain in his chest tightened, making it difficult to breathe. He stopped short and forced a deep breath.

"Taggart! There you are, man. We've been waiting."

Finn's blood ran cold. The reason for his rejection of Lucy stood before him, impatiently waiting for Finn to catch up. Finn shoved his emotions back into the deep, dark hole inside his heart and turned to his employer. Philip Halford was an up-and-coming politician who had brilliant prospects in the mayoral election. Finn also owed the man his life, and therefore, his servitude. At least for the time being.

The man was the epitome of society: well-bred, civic-minded, philanthropic. Outwardly. Those in the right circles knew nothing of his murky past and he paid a lot of money to keep it that way. And now Finn was serving as his right-hand man. Finn had a feeling that Halford wanted to keep him close so he could watch him, more than any other reason. After the kidnapping fiasco in Boston, Halford had decided Finn's talents would be of more use to him personally than out in the field. Finn didn't agree. But he had little choice in the matter. Halford owned him, for all intents and purposes, for another two years.

So far, the job had been relatively easy. Finn had been helping with Halford's campaign, overseeing the odd shipment or two when Halford had cargo coming in he wanted to keep secret, and occasionally he acted as a sort of bodyguard, keeping fans and detractors alike from getting too close to the politician. Though, in truth, nothing remotely dangerous had ever occurred. In fact, Finn often felt he should be guarding the public from Halford, rather than the other way around. The man took the whole political game a little too seriously. No old lady or baby within a mile of Halford was safe. And that was just the face he showed the public. If his true nature were ever revealed…well, it would take more than Finn to keep the man from a noose.

But now that Lucy had found Finn, something would have to be done. He'd just have to make her see reason, get her to return home. Though he was laughing at that thought even before it had been fully formed. Lucy was just as stubborn as her sisters. Perhaps even more so. As the baby of a trio of formidable women, she'd had to fight to get her voice heard. As a result, she was almost impossible to deter once her mind was set.

And she knew where he was now. It would probably be best, be easiest for both of them, if he disappeared again. The thought of leaving her sent another shard of anguish through his heart. He'd barely been able to turn his back on her the first time. Just now, leaving her in that hotel room had ripped open the scar on his heart and left a gaping, bleeding wound. How could he stand his ground and make her leave if she persisted, as he greatly feared she would?

He'd have to. He was no good for her and had nothing to offer. She might not care about his background or his lack of money, but society certainly would. And even more importantly, her family would never allow it. Brynne would flay him alive if she ever saw him again, no matter what Lucy said, and he couldn't really blame her. He had kidnapped Brynne's daughter. But he'd kept her safe from the smugglers he'd worked for—as safe and as happy as possible. If he hadn't taken her, one of his associates would have. Finn shuddered to think what Coraline's treatment would have been under their care.

But even if Brynne understood that, he doubted she'd forgiven him. She'd certainly never forget. And Lucy was too close to her sisters for their opinions to not matter to her. Even worse, if Lucy stayed, she'd be noticed by Halford. Lucy was beautiful, unattached, and rich. She'd be irresistible to his boss. He'd been looking for a wealthy wife for a while and though he'd prefer one a little more gently bred than Lucy, he'd overlook that for her fortune.

Finn could not let Halford get his hooks into her. No one would ever be good enough for Lucy but Halford was the worst sort of scoundrel. A criminal who masqueraded as the best society had to offer. Finn had once seen him break a man's legs for failing to repay a debt and then return to a party with his politician's grin on his face as though nothing had happened. He'd taken a man's wife as mistress in lieu of payment on a deal, cheated orphans and widows out of their inheritances, ruthlessly pursued what he wanted and had trafficked in slavery, murder, mayhem, and misery. And those were just a few of the things Finn knew of. Halford was a black-hearted fiend, through and through.

It would be best if Finn left. Went somewhere Lucy could never find him. Where her association with him couldn't hurt her. Perhaps he could try Australia. Or India. If it weren't for Halford, that's exactly what he'd do. But he owed Halford. And he wasn't going to be allowed to forget that.

"Taggart?"

Finn jerked, startled out of his thoughts. Halford stood looking at him, his brow furrowed. "Are you all right, man?"

Finn straightened. "Yes, of course. My apologies." He held his hand out, trying to lead Halford out the door. Finn wanted him out of the hotel before Lucy came downstairs.

"Is everything set for my speech?"

"Yes. I've done a thorough search of the venue. Everything is set up and secure and I have two of my men stationed inside making sure it stays that way. I'll have the carriage waiting for you at the back entrance to bring you back to the hotel as soon as you are through."

"Good, good. Though I thought I should take a few moments to mingle with the crowd afterward. Give them some personal attention. Kiss a few babies and all that. Must give the people what they want, eh?" Halford chuckled and Finn stifled a sigh. The man was an abject bore.

"I don't think that would be wise, sir. I cannot guarantee who will be in the audience and therefore cannot guarantee your safety—"

"Nonsense. With you at my side, I have no fears. Now, shall we be off?"

"Yes, sir," Finn said, resigned to another long afternoon

of watching the politician swindling his way through another crowd of voters.

"Finn!"

Finn's stomach dropped.

"Finn!"

Lucy had made her way down the stairs and was marching purposely toward them. Finn tried to ignore her. He turned his back, hoping he blocked the view of her, and tried to steer Halford out the door but Halford was looking over his shoulder at Lucy with an interest that made Finn's blood burn.

"Well, now. Who is this delightful creature?" Halford asked as Lucy caught up with them.

Finn fumed, his jaw locked tight, anger and a thread of fear pumping through him. Lucy looked from him to Halford, obviously waiting to be introduced. When Finn didn't say anything she turned her pert little chin up in the air and addressed him herself.

"Pleased to make your acquaintance, sir. I'm — "

"This is my cousin," Finn interjected. "Lucy."

Lucy frowned up at him, confusion and hurt shadowing her eyes. Finn was sorry to cause her more pain, but she needed to understand that there was nothing between them. And he couldn't allow Halford to know how much Lucy meant to him. Couldn't give him any more leverage to use against him. Making her his cousin kept their true relationship secret and kept her real identity hidden. Hopefully, Halford would assume she was as unworthy as Finn and undeserving of his interest.

"Shame on you, Taggart! You never told me you had such an enchanting cousin. Tell me, my dear, are you in town visiting, or do you live in our fair city? Though surely you must be visiting for I am certain I would have made your acquaintance before now had you been in Charlotte for any amount of time."

Lucy gave Halford a polite smile. "I just came into town to visit my cousin," she said, her nose wrinkling a bit at the word. "I'd only just heard he was here. We lost contact during the war."

"Of course, of course. Such a shame you lost touch," Halford said, eyeing Finn thoughtfully. "But how delightful to finally meet up again! Well, you must certainly join us. Do you have any plans this afternoon?"

"Yes," Finn interrupted. "I believe my cousin needs to pack her belongings. She is returning home first thing in the morning."

Lucy glared at him.

"Oh, that's a shame," Halford said, his shrewd eyes darting between them, though he played oblivious to the tension burning between the two. "I don't suppose I could convince you to stay longer? I'm just on my way to deliver what I believe will be a very enlightening speech and I will be hosting a ball in just a few weeks at my home. It would be wonderful if you could attend."

"I'm afraid she can't—"

"Why, that sounds wonderful!" Lucy said, ignoring Finn. "I was just telling Finn that I wished I could stay a bit longer and now I have the perfect excuse. I'm sure my family wouldn't mind if I prolonged my visit."

"Wonderful!" Halford exclaimed. "Would you care to accompany us? It would be my pleasure to escort you." He offered Lucy his elbow, his greedy gaze devouring her in a way that made Finn want to pummel the man.

"That would be delightful, thank you." Lucy took Halford's elbow, threw a triumphant look over her shoulder at Finn, and allowed Halford to lead her out the door to the waiting carriage.

Just perfect. Dread settled into a hard, icy knot in his gut. Not only had he *not* succeeded in getting Lucy to leave, but she had firmly ensconced herself in the lion's den. She had no idea who she was dealing with and Finn needed to enlighten her. In the meantime, he was going to have the dubious pleasure of watching as she was squired around town by the man he was working for. Which meant Finn would be forced to witness every smarmy move on Halford's part. And Finn would be in Lucy's company. Every day.

His sanity would never survive.

. . .

The carriage pulled up in front of a small courtyard of a run-down factory where a platform had been constructed. Lucy was taken aback at the location. She'd expected Mr. Halford would be addressing a group of upper-class men, perhaps in an upscale club or a supporter's mansion or some such place. But the crowd already milling around in front of the stage consisted of largely middle-to lower-class whites. Lucy was surprised to see quite a few black faces among the throng, considering the fact that it was not yet legal for them to vote in this part of the country.

She clambered down from the carriage gratefully. The tension inside had been thicker than frozen molasses with Finn glowering at her the entire way. Well, tough for him. Despite what he said, Lucy didn't believe that he truly wanted her to go away. That kiss when he'd first seen her…Lucy's heart skipped a beat at the mere memory. He loved her, she was sure of it. She just had to make the stubborn ass admit it. And to do that she'd need to stick around.

Mr. Halford held out his arm with a gallant smile and Lucy once again took it, letting him draw her into his side. Finn's look darkened, his jaw clenching so tightly his lips almost disappeared. Well, maybe a little jealousy would help things along. After all, surely he wouldn't stand by and let her be courted by someone else. And whiling away a few hours with the charming Mr. Halford might be amusing. He seemed pleasant enough and he was certainly handsome. Lucy could think of worse ways to spend her time.

Finn turned away and scanned the crowd while Mr. Halford deposited Lucy near the front. She watched the gathering assembly with interest. There were a good many angry faces among the waiting spectators, which was curious, as the speech hadn't yet begun. Finn's voice at her elbow made her jump.

"Some of Mr. Halford's ideas are a bit unpopular with the public. Well, with the upper-class white public, at any rate."

Lucy turned to Finn with interest. "Oh. And what would those be?"

"He advocates voting rights for everyone, regardless of race or social status. Including former slaves."

"Everyone? Even women?"

"I should have said all males. Even he isn't that progressive."

Lucy snorted. "Well, it's something, I suppose. Better than most politicians in the area, I'd imagine."

"Oh, don't mistake his policies for his actual beliefs. He's just a bit more shrewd than most. It's a huge, untapped voter population. If he's popular with them, and they turn out in droves to vote, he's almost guaranteed to win."

Lucy cocked her head as she gazed at him. "You don't seem to like your employer much."

"I loathe him."

Lucy's eyes widened and Finn shrugged, his attention on Mr. Halford as the man mounted the stage. "Whether I like him or not is irrelevant. I was hired to be his errand boy and occasional bodyguard. I don't have to like him for that."

Lucy followed his gaze. "Shouldn't you be up there with him?"

"He doesn't wish to appear fearful. I can keep an eye on things from down here. And another of Halford's men is on the platform with him. Mr. Halford is paranoid and self-serving. He wouldn't be up there right now if he thought he was in true danger."

"Rather cynical of you, Mr. Taggart."

Finn's gaze met hers and Lucy fought to breathe. She wanted nothing more than to throw herself in his arms and beg him to love her. But his private rejection had been miserable enough. She certainly had no intention of forcing a repeat performance in public.

"Not cynical. Realistic. I prefer to keep my feet firmly planted in reality, not bury my head in the sand and only see what I want to see."

"And why do I get the feeling we aren't discussing Mr. Halford anymore?"

"You need to go home, Lucy. Nothing you do will convince me to change my mind. Staying here will only mean more heartache. Go home."

Lucy looked away, clenching her jaw against the anguish burning its way up her throat. When she could speak without blubbering like a heartsick fool, she answered him, though she kept her gaze glued to the stage. "I have no intention of returning home just yet. I've never been to Charlotte. I should really make the most of my visit while I'm here." Her eyes focused on Mr. Halford. "Besides, you aren't the only dog on the prairie, Finnegan Taggart. If you don't want me, there are other men who might."

Mr. Halford caught her gaze and aimed a charming smile and bow in her direction before moving his attention back to his rapt audience. Lucy looked up at Finn, gratified to see he'd caught their exchange, and didn't seem to be at all pleased about it. "Why shouldn't I stick around and see what might come of it? There's nothing for me in Boston."

Finn grabbed her arm and pulled her to the side, away from any prying ears. "Lucy, Halford is not someone you should be getting involved with. You need to stay away from him."

"Why, Finn? Tell me the real reason you don't want me to see him." Lucy held her breath, hoping and praying he'd just fess up and tell her he loved her and couldn't stand to see her with another man.

Finn's eyes drifted from hers down to her mouth, lingered. He leaned a fraction of an inch closer and Lucy held her breath. She wanted to press closer, close the distance between them. He wanted to kiss her again; she knew it. Could feel it in the sudden tension in him, the way his grip tightened slightly on her arm, the slight hitch in his breathing.

Then Finn glanced toward the stage. Lucy followed his gaze and saw Mr. Halford briefly frown between the two of them before plastering a grin back on his face. Finn let go of her arm.

"I can't discuss it here. Suffice it to say, he's not right for you."

Lucy forced down the tears that threatened to erupt and straightened her backbone. "Well, by your own choice, my personal life is no longer any of your business. I'll see whomever I wish to see. Now, if you'll excuse me."

Lucy moved closer to the stage and watched the crowd as Mr. Halford spoke. There were a few faces, those belonging to the more affluent men, Lucy noted, who glowered menacingly at Mr. Halford as he spoke. But the majority of the crowd watched him with interest.

Lucy forced a smile to her face when Mr. Halford winked down at her. No matter what she wanted Finn to think, she'd never be able to replace him. Mr. Halford was handsome, powerful, rich, and well connected. Everything a girl should want. And Lucy didn't feel even a spark of attraction to him.

Yet, if Finn had his way, she'd have to learn how to live without him. She didn't know if she could. She'd managed to survive for the last several years by withdrawing into herself. Staying numb, detached. But one look at Finn had blown her carefully crafted facade to bits. It was as though her heart had finally begun beating again.

And with its reawakening came the pain shredding through it. If Finn had his way, that would be something she'd need to learn to live with as well. Because she couldn't imagine it being whole without him.

Chapter Six

Lucy took a deep breath, enjoying the cool morning air before the heat of the late summer set in. The park across from the hotel was nearly empty this early in the morning and Lucy was happy to be able to wander unimpeded while she contemplated her predicament.

She'd been in Charlotte for two weeks now and she'd made no headway with Finn. The stubborn man still kept his distance from her, though she didn't think he was as unaffected by her as he tried to pretend.

And a new complication was arising. Philip Halford. Since Lucy spent most of her time sticking as close to Finn as possible, and Finn was Philip's right-hand man, she had been seeing a lot more of Philip than she'd expected. Philip, much to Lucy's surprise, seemed delighted by her presence. Compared to Finn's continued rejection of her, it was a bit of a balm to her spirit to have an attractive man seek her company, even if she did not return his interest.

Lucy meandered back to the hotel and was brought up short by the sight of Finn descending the steps toward a waiting carriage. He looked up and caught her gaze. For a moment, Lucy thought he'd continue on his way without a word to her, but instead, he came toward her.

Lucy watched him approach, her eyes drinking in every inch of him, the way his trousers hugged his legs, the snug fit of his vest and coat over his toned physique. She could very happily spend hours just watching him. He came to a stop in front of her and neither said anything for a moment.

Finally, Lucy nodded toward the carriage. "Are you going somewhere?"

Finn nodded. "Halford has a few tasks for me out of the city."

Lucy tried not to show her disappointment. "How long will you be gone?"

"A week. Maybe two."

"Oh." She looked down at the grass beneath her feet. Lucy didn't want him to go. She'd only just found him and the thought of him being away sent a rush of panic through her that she had a hard time controlling.

"Lucy, I—"

"Taggart?" Lucy and Finn looked toward the hotel to see Philip standing beside the carriage. When he caught sight of them, he hurried over. "There you are, man. You always seem to be disappearing on me. Quite annoying, I must say," Philip said with a good-natured laugh.

Lucy knew how he felt, though she didn't feel particularly jovial about it.

"I was just saying good-bye to my cousin."

"Ah yes," Philip said, turning his attention to Lucy. "The charming Miss Taggart. Well, never you fear. Finnegan will return shortly. In the meantime, I'd be delighted to help take charge of you. In fact, I'm attending a small musical soiree this evening. I'd be honored if you'd accompany me."

Lucy hesitated and looked at Finn. Every line of his face

was taut, his nostrils flaring slightly, though he was careful to show no real expression. A surge of irritation hit her and she made a snap decision. If Finn wanted to continue this charade, then she could too. Besides, she saw no reason why she should confine herself to her hotel room, pining over Finn while he was gone.

"I'd be delighted, Mr. Halford. Thank you."

"It will be my pleasure, my dear. Well then, I'll be by to fetch you at seven o'clock this evening, if that is acceptable."

"I'll be ready."

"Excellent." Philip turned his attention to Finn. "Taggart, you'd better be on your way, hadn't you?"

Finn pinned Lucy with a glare that, far from his intention, she was sure, made Lucy bite her lip to keep from grinning. Then he smiled at her and stepped closer, grasping both her arms as he pulled her to him. "Be well, *cousin*," he said. He kissed her cheek, letting his lips linger a fraction longer than was polite. He pulled back slowly, keeping his cheek pressed against hers for as long as possible. "I shall see you when I return."

His eyes burned into hers and she pulled back a bit, startled by the intensity. "Take care, Lucy."

Lucy nodded dumbly, unable to come up with a single coherent retort. Finn's chuckle as he hopped into the carriage broke the spell and she glared after him. Then again, she'd definitely gotten a reaction out of him. One she quite enjoyed. If agreeing to a simple soiree aggravated him this much, she'd have to make it a point to attend a few more.

• • •

Lucy sat before her vanity table while Lilah, a maid the hotel had found for her, dressed her hair. She'd been kept busy lately as Philip had been squiring her all over town. She enjoyed his company more than she'd anticipated. He was charming, funny, and flirtatious. She found it surprisingly enjoyable. Still, she missed Finn. He'd been away nearly two weeks and Lucy was in a fever of anticipation to see him again.

Tonight, Lucy was accompanying Philip to a ball he was hosting. It was apparently one of *the* social events of the season and everyone of any note would be attending. Though Lucy only cared about Finn. Philip had mentioned that Finn had returned. If he was going to be at the ball, she wanted to make sure she looked her best.

The thought of seeing Finn again brought a blush to her cheeks. Lilah caught sight of it.

"Your young man won't be able to take his eyes off you."

Startled, Lucy met the maid's eyes in the mirror. "Pardon?"

"Nothin' puts a blush to a girl's cheeks like the thought of her love." Lilah winked at her and turned her attention back to the strands of hair she was braiding.

Nothing would make her happier than to see Finn's face alight with pleasure upon seeing her. But she knew that wouldn't happen. Even if he appreciated her appearance, he'd most likely frown and glower as always. Why did she keep torturing herself? She was growing fonder of Philip. Perhaps she should give up on Finn and try to move on with her life.

But she didn't think she could.

"No, I don't...I don't have...he doesn't..." Lucy was horrified to hear the hitch in her voice. Tears burned behind her eyes, and for the first time in weeks, they spilled over, running down her cheeks.

"Oh, Miz Lucy! I'm so sorry. I shore didn't aim to upset you."

"No, no, it's not your fault." Lucy took a deep, shuddering breath. "It's just...oh, I've just bungled everything."

Lilah listened intently as Lucy filled her in on the complexities of her relationship with Finn, and the added complication of Philip.

When Lucy had finished, Lilah pursed her lips, her deft hands weaving in and out of Lucy's hair.

"Well I hope you pardon my say so, miss, but why are you still hankerin' for a man who says he doesn't want you?"

Lucy laughed, though there was no happiness in the sound. "Yes, that is the question, isn't it?"

She didn't answer for a moment and then finally shrugged. "I love him. I've always loved him. And I can't imagine ever not loving him. When he left, he took a part of me. And now that I've found him again…it's as though I'm whole once more. As melodramatic as this will sound," she said with a wry smile, "I was merely existing when he was gone. And now that he's here, I feel alive again. Like I'm finally myself. I can't go back to the way things were. I can't live like that anymore. And despite what he says, I think he still loves me, too. Whatever his reasons for not wanting me here, I don't think a lack of love is one of them."

"Well, then. I suppose you have yo' answer."

Lucy's mouth opened to protest. But she couldn't make the words come out. Lilah was right. There were only two options. Go back to Boston, back to her old life. Or stay, and try and talk some sense into Finn. And the first option wasn't really an option.

She nodded. "Fight it is, then."

Lilah placed her hands on Lucy's shoulders and turned Lucy on the stool so she was looking full in the mirror. "I think the battle is more than half won already, miss, if'n I do say so myself. Even if the man had no feelin's for you, he'd be sore pressed to resist you tonight."

Lucy's stomach somersaulted. "Well, I don't know about that. But I'm going to do my damn level best to make Finn remember what he's missing."

"Finn? Finnegan Taggart?"

"Yes. Do you know him?" Lucy asked, surprised.

"Yes, miss. Very well. He's a mighty fine man. You couldn't do better and that's the God's honest truth."

"I agree, but I hope you don't mind my asking why you think so. How do you know him?"

Lilah looked down, her face carefully blank. "I run a school. At night. I teach folks how to read a little, write some."

"I think that's wonderful," Lucy said, giving the maid a warm smile.

"You do?"

"Of course. I'm sure there's a great need for that."

"Oh yes, miss, there surely is. My first master let me be educated with his daughter. She never wanted to sit with her tutor, but if I was there, she'd behave all right. So I got to learn right along with her. And now, well, I thought, if'n I could help others learn, maybe that could help their circumstances. They could go up north maybe, get jobs. Somethin' better'n what they got."

"And Finn?"

"He helps me sometimes. Comes in and helps teach. There's so many that want to learn and I only know a little. Don't have room to teach many neither. So they take turns. Some come one week, some another. Mr. Taggart, he comes in a couple times a week and helps out when he can."

Lucy's heart warmed. That sounded like the Finn she'd known. "Well you sound like you could use some more help. I'd be happy to assist in any way that I can."

Lilah's mouth dropped open. "Oh, Miz Lucy, that would be wonderful. Truly. But surely you don't have time."

Lucy laughed. "Actually, I've got nothing but time. Until our dear Mr. Taggart warms to the idea of me being here, I have no intention of leaving. But the last thing I want to do is sit around the hotel all day. I'd love to do something useful with my time, and I can't imagine anything more worthwhile than helping to educate those who need it."

"You…you understand that the folks I teach…they…they former slaves. All of them."

"Well yes, I assumed as much."

"And that don't bother you none?"

"Should it?"

Lilah's face went carefully blank again. "There's a lot of folks out here that want things back the way they were. They don't take very kindly to those who tryin' to change things up, no matter what the laws might say now."

"Well, those people can just go kiss my great-aunt Fanny. I do what I like and there is nothing more that I'd like than to help you with your school."

Lilah nodded with a cautious grin. "We'd sure be grateful."

"Wonderful! Well, how about tomorrow morning we can go down to this school of yours and have a look-see."

Lilah's face fell. "I work at the hotel during the days. That's why folks only come by at night."

"You let me take care of that. I'm sure the hotel will agree to let me hire you out for the remainder of my stay. I'll just tell them I have need of a lady's maid. I'm sure they will be accommodating."

"If Mr. Taggart don't just fall at your feet, that man is a fool."

Lucy laughed. "On that, we agree."

She stood and took one last look in the mirror. "Well, let's see if we can get our stubborn Mr. Taggart to see reason."

Lilah smiled and Lucy took a deep breath.

• • •

Lucy spun in Philip's arms, the room whirring by her in a kaleidoscope of colors and sounds. All the laughing women, the grinning men, the fancy dresses with their enormous hoops, flew past her vision in a blur. One face stood out. One smoldering, fuming face stood out from all the rest. Would always stand out. But his bad humor was his own fault.

It was obvious, from the way Finn had been glowering at them all night that he'd heard about her little excursions with Philip while he'd been away. She'd made sure they'd been seen together often enough. Or if that wasn't the case, Finn was at the very least, unhappy about how comfortable she seemed with Philip. Or maybe he was just nursing the old gripe that she'd ignored his wishes and stayed in town for the single purpose of attending this ball.

Well…tough beans for him. They hadn't had an opportunity to speak in private again since he'd returned, so she had no idea what his exact complaints against Philip were and at the moment, she didn't care. She hadn't seen any untoward behavior, nothing that raised any alarms. In fact, even though she'd never feel for Philip what she felt for Finn, she rather enjoyed his company. She even found it pleasant being in his arms, though the slight warmth she felt in Philip's embrace did not come close to the smoldering burn that scorched her with a mere look from Finn.

But if Finn didn't want her with Philip, all he had to do to was admit that he loved her. She wasn't asking for much. She didn't care if they married or not. She'd very happily live in sin with him for the rest of her mortal days. Burning in hell would be worth it if she could spend her life in Finn's arms. Not that she believed they'd suffer those consequences. The worst that would befall them would be possible ostracism from society. And society, in Lucy's humble opinion, could take a flying leap into a cactus patch. She'd gladly give up her good name if it meant being with Finn.

Whatever catastrophic issues Finn thought he had, she would deal with. Why couldn't the stubborn man just see that if he'd let her help him, his life would be so much better?

"Stubborn mule," Lucy muttered.

"Pardon me, my dear?" Philip asked, leaning in to better hear her.

"Oh, nothing. I think I could use a bit of air, couldn't you?"

"Ah," Philip said with a chuckle. "It is rather warm in here. Shall we venture out into the gardens for a moment?"

"Oh yes, let's," Lucy said, smiling up at him. She threw a quick glance over her shoulder at Finn, who, as usual, was right on their heels.

They stepped out onto the terrace and Lucy took a deep breath of the cool night air. Philip placed his hand on her lower back to guide her toward the steps and Lucy could have sworn she heard Finn's jaw popping, he was clenching so hard.

Serves him right. She stifled the twinge of guilt she felt for using Mr. Halford to make Finn jealous. Though Lucy had no illusions that Philip was truly interested in her. After all, who was she? As far as Philip knew, she was merely the cousin of his employee. Hardly a suitable companion for someone from such an old family, someone who could very likely be sitting in the White House conversing with President Johnson in the near future.

From what she'd heard, Philip always had some pretty young thing on his arm, each more beautiful and richer than the last. She didn't fit into his frame of interest, at least as far as he was aware, so Lucy didn't know why he seemed so eager for her company. She didn't care to know, truth to tell. His interest gave her a convenient way to stay close to Finn, so his suitability as a potential match was irrelevant. He seemed to genuinely enjoy her company, but Lucy was very certain his attentions, his honorable ones at any rate, didn't stretch further than that.

They spent a few moments strolling about garden paths lit with colorful lanterns. Servants in brightly colored dresses and handsome suits wandered among the guests offering refreshments.

"Oh, there's Judge Thomas. I really should say, hello. The old curmudgeon hardly ever pries himself from his comfortable armchair. He'd be quite put out if I didn't make a fuss over him."

Philip deposited Lucy on a bench and bent to kiss her hand. "Now, don't go running off, now. You sit right there and have some refreshments," he waved a girl over, "and I'll be back before you even have time to miss me."

"Oh, I don't know about that," Lucy simpered.

Finn stared at her, his eyebrows raised. All right, perhaps she was laying it on a bit thick. But Philip didn't seem to notice. He simply smiled, kissed her hand again, and hurried off.

"I don't know what game you are playing at, but it's revolting." Finn stood beside her, his gaze moving around the crowd, never lingering on her for too long.

"Who says I'm playing?"

"Philip Halford is not the type of man you want to trifle with. You need to go have fun elsewhere. Preferably back in Boston where your sisters can keep an eye on you."

Lucy rolled her eyes. "I am not a child. I don't need anyone to keep an eye on me. Besides, I assure you, I'm not having any fun. Mr. Halford is a means to an end. And don't start lecturing me about that either. You and I both know there isn't a genuine bone in his politician's body. Especially not where a pretty face is concerned. So no one is going to get hurt here."

Finn just shook his head. "I have half a mind to tell your sisters what you are up to, so they can come fetch you back home."

Lucy felt a momentary qualm at his threat but stamped it down. "They already know what I'm up to. They are fully aware I came down here to find you. Besides, you wouldn't dare contact Brynne. You're afraid she'll skin you alive if she were to ever clap eyes on you again. You're more scared of her than I am."

Finn snorted, but he didn't deny it. Both of her sisters were fierce on the best of days. But Finn had crossed an unspoken line when he'd kidnapped Brynne's daughter, no matter what his reasons. Finn was lucky he'd escaped her wrath the first time. He'd never willingly face her again, especially since he knew he deserved her fury.

Lucy took a small cake from the serving girl Philip had summoned and thanked her with a smile. The girl gave her a quick curtsy and moved off.

Lucy lifted the cake to her lips and bit down just as Finn leaned down to speak in her ear.

"They used to be his slaves, you know."

Lucy inhaled a cake crumb and had to cough a few times to dislodge it from her throat. She'd known Philip must have had slaves, of course. This was North Carolina. Practically anyone with any sort of means did. Still, being confronted with it was a bit startling.

"They aren't slaves any longer."

"They aren't much better. Just because the laws changed doesn't mean they are enforced. And changed laws don't change people's beliefs. I'm surprised you are courting a man who owned slaves."

Lucy shifted on the hard bench, brushing invisible crumbs from her skirt. "We aren't courting."

A couple passing by glanced at Finn and Lucy, their faces alight with amused curiosity, obviously assuming the two were having a lovers' tiff. Which, Lucy supposed, they were.

"Why are you mentioning all this?" she asked.

"Because if you are determined to continue with this game you are playing, I want you to understand who it is you are playing with. You are toying with a man who felt, and still feels, I might add, no matter what he says in his pretty speeches, that it is his right to own other human beings. A man whose sole purpose in life, at the moment, is to convince a state of like-minded men to vote him into a position of power so he can fight for their right to continue their way of life down here. And I am not just speaking of his servants. Halford uses any means necessary to get what he wants and that includes the people in his life. You have no idea what type of man he really is, what he's capable of. And you are treating him like he's some green boy in a misguided attempt to make me jealous."

Lucy's growing trepidation at Finn's words made her anxious, but she shoved her unease down deep and focused on the last part of his statement.

"If it *is* a game I'm playing, I'm doing it rather well, I think. You *are* jealous, aren't you?"

Finn blew out an exasperated breath. "You are acting like a ridiculous, childish brat, refusing to do what's best for you because it's not what you want. You have no care for anyone else's feelings in this matter. Not mine, not even Halford's, if the man were capable of any. I'm just waiting for you to stamp your little foot and proclaim that life is unfair."

Lucy flinched from the anger in Finn's voice, from the derision in his eyes. Is that how he really saw her? As a spoiled child? Ridiculous?

Hurt and embarrassment flooded through her, made worse by the fact that he wasn't wrong. She was being childish. No matter what Philip's true feelings toward her, it didn't excuse her behavior toward him. She honestly didn't know what was coming over her. It was like seeing Finn again had completely erased all common sense and decency in her, leaving her a raw, emotional mess that would do anything to anyone as long as it meant spending one more day with her love.

She didn't know how much longer she could take it. Neither her so-called relationship with Philip or Finn's continued rejection. She couldn't let Finn go without a fight. But how long could she fight before she'd have to admit that there wasn't anything there worth fighting for? The thought made her stomach churn.

"All right. Maybe I am being ridiculous, and yes, I do think that life is unfair. What a colossal joke. I fall in love with an amazing, wonderful man who is too stubborn to see just how incredible he is, who disappears from my life. Then I spend seven years not knowing if he's dead or alive. Finally, by some miracle, I find him again, and he's too damn stubborn to admit that he still loves me! So I'm forced into playing childish, ridiculous games just so I can spend another five minutes in his company."

She looked down at the small cake she'd crumbled in her hands, defeat dragging at her heart. "Maybe you are right. Maybe it would be best if I just went home, left you in peace. Maybe it would have been better if I'd just gone on assuming you were dead."

"Lucy," Finn said, his wide eyes staring into hers. "I'm truly sorry if you are hurt. If I could take your pain away, I would."

Lucy clenched her hands into fists, the urge to beat some sense into him so strong she trembled with it. "You could take it away! You just refuse to do so. Why can't you just admit you love me? And don't give me your nonsense about not being good enough. I am perfectly capable of deciding who is worthy of me."

"Lucy…" Finn spread his hands wide, as though he were trying to calm a spooked horse. But he didn't make any attempt to answer her.

"Damn it, Finn! Maybe you don't even know how to love, because you sure as hell make it impossible for anyone to love you."

The second the words were out of Lucy's mouth, she wished she could yank them back. For a moment, Finn sat stunned, hurt flashing through his eyes. She'd never said anything so hateful, so mean, in her whole life. And she'd never meant anything less.

"Finn, I'm sorry, I didn't mean it. My God, I love you so much I can barely breathe when we are apart. I've scarcely existed these last seven years and then I found you and it's as if I've woken from a nightmare. I just…the thought of going back to that hellish half-life has me crazed."

No matter the pain he'd caused her, it was no excuse for saying something so cruel to him. How often had her heart broken over the thought of the man she loved being alone in the world? It was one of the reasons she'd been so determined to find him. And yet there she sat, throwing his sorrows back in his face.

Maybe she didn't deserve him after all.

"I'm sorry," she whispered. She stood to go.

"I've loved two women in my life," he said, so faintly Lucy almost didn't hear him.

"What?"

Finn gazed off into the distance, in the direction of Philip, though Lucy didn't think he saw him.

"The first was a very long time ago. It…didn't end well." Finn turned to look at Lucy. "Then there was you. And that didn't end well, either," he said with a sad smile.

Lucy sat back down. "It doesn't have to end."

Finn stared into her eyes, his mouth slightly open as though he'd refute that, but he didn't say anything. His gaze dropped to her lips for a moment before meeting her eyes again. Lucy's breath quickened and she leaned ever so slightly closer. She wanted to encourage him without spooking him. Even in her own mind that sounded ridiculous. She felt like she was out to seduce some unwilling virgin. The thought almost made her smile. Then Finn bit his bottom lip and leaned in.

Lucy's head swam and she closed her eyes, waiting for the touch of Finn's lips. His breath brushed across her cheek.

Philip's braying laugh rang out across the courtyard and Lucy's eyes flew open. Finn was looking at her with a mixture of disappointment and alarm.

Philip began walking back toward them and Finn stood, his face going blank as he stepped back into his guard persona.

"Finn."

He shook his head with a stubborn frown, his attention fixed on the approaching Philip. "We'll talk later. This isn't a game. You don't understand the danger you're in."

"Wha—"

Philip stopped before her, looking between them with a cocked brow, effectively cutting off any further conversation. "Sorry to abandon you so long, my dear. Shall we go back inside?"

Lucy forced a smile to her lips. "Yes, of course."

She looped her hand through Philip's offered arm and let him lead her back to the ballroom. She glanced over her shoulder and was startled to meet Finn's burning gaze. There was a renewed determination in his eyes and Lucy knew her fight to make him see reason had just intensified.

But he'd been about to kiss her. Lucy was sure of it.

Perhaps all was not lost after all.

Chapter Seven

Lucy glanced at Finn from the corner of her eye as he escorted her to her room in the hotel. They had shared a carriage with another couple who had come into Charlotte just for Philip's ball. So Lucy had no chance to question Finn on his dire warnings. Honestly, his attitude was beginning to wear on her nerves. Since the close call in the courtyard, Finn had gone out of his way to not touch her. Not even when doing so was expected. He'd held the carriage door open for her, but had made no move to help her inside, leaving her to clamber in unassisted. He'd sat beside her in the carriage but had kept his gaze fixed on the window, never once turning in her direction and holding himself so stiffly he didn't even brush against her skirts. Quite a feat considering the size of them.

Upon arriving at the hotel, the other couple descended, gave them a polite nod, and went on their way. Lucy hopped down after them, leaving Finn in the carriage. She had no wish for a repeat performance and didn't want to wait in the carriage to see if he'd offer her his hand. Part of her was afraid that if he did and she took it, she'd never let it go. The other part of her was afraid he wouldn't offer it at all. Best to beat him to the draw and just get out of the blasted carriage herself.

She hiked her skirts and took the steps of the hotel two at a time. Finn was right on her heels, but she ignored him. She was suddenly very weary. All the near misses, the what-ifs and guesswork, were wearing on her nerves and her patience. Lucy was certain he still wanted her. Whether or not he still loved her...that was more difficult to ascertain, though Lucy was willing to bet he did. His continued denial of that fact was getting on her last nerve. And the push and pull of her emotions with every almost kiss or significant eye contact was shredding what was left of her sanity. And dignity.

For the first time in her life, she might have to give up the fight. Enough was enough. Life was too short to waste it on such nonsense.

Lucy had always done what needed doing and didn't give much thought to those who might not approve. She saw no point in hemming and hawing over anything. It had saved her a lot of indecision and guilt in her life. Things were usually fairly cut and dry for her. Lucy hadn't liked herself or her behavior in recent weeks.

But Finn had always been the exception to her rules. He was patently unsuitable for her in every way most thought important...and yet she'd never met anyone more suited for her. He was a walking conflict. A complicated conflict at that. One who insisted he didn't want her. And had he been anyone else, Lucy wouldn't have bothered with him.

But he was Finn. Her Finn.

And not bothering hadn't been an option. Perhaps that was changing.

They'd reached her door. She turned to face him. "Come inside."

Finn started, his eyes glancing up and down the hallway. A few people wandered about, going in or out of their rooms.

"I don't think that would be wise."

"You said we needed to talk, and you aren't willing to do it anywhere we might be overheard. If my room is unacceptable, then perhaps you'd be more comfortable if we went to yours."

"As we would still be in the hotel, I don't see how that would be any more suitable."

Lucy frowned. "Well, since you don't have any other place we can go, I don't see any other options. Why are you living in a hotel, anyway? Wouldn't you prefer to have a place of your own?"

Finn shrugged. "It's more convenient. Halford often travels. Living here allows me to come and go as I need without having to worry about a home to care for. My needs are taken care of without having to hire staff."

"And it means you have nothing to tie you to this place if you decided to leave in a hurry."

Finn didn't acknowledge that comment directly, but did answer, "As I said, it's convenient."

"Well, fine then. It's late. I'm tired. Unless you want to speak your peace out here in the open, I don't see that we have another choice. If you don't want to come to my room, then I'll just come to yours."

An older couple passing by glanced at them, the woman's mouth puckered disapprovingly. Lucy just widened her eyes and gave the woman her most innocent smile. As soon as they'd passed she muttered, "Nosy old biddy."

"Nosy or not, she's the perfect example of why you can't come to my room," Finn said. "If you were seen entering or leaving it, your reputation would be in ruins."

Lucy shrugged. "You are the one with all the dire secrets and an infuriating need for privacy. Keep them to yourself, if you prefer. I'm going to bed. Philip has asked me to accompany him to the theater tomorrow evening and I need to get some rest."

Lucy turned her back on Finn and entered her room. "Good night," she said with a smile. Then she closed the door on his glowering face.

. . .

Finn walked past Lucy's door. Stopped. Turned around. Walked past it again. Finally, he came to a stop in front of it, his hand raised to turn the knob. It was very late. Or early. They hadn't returned from the ball until well after midnight and he'd been tossing and turning for an hour at least before finally deciding he couldn't wait any longer to warn Lucy. She was being extraordinarily stubborn, even for a Richardson, and that was saying something.

He'd thought, hoped, that she'd have given up on him long before now. But the stubborn little minx wasn't backing down. The problem was, she was right. About everything. He did still love her. So much that the mere sight of her made his chest burn with a bittersweet longing that he'd give almost anything to quench. Almost anything. But not her safety. He didn't know if he could protect her against Halford and he'd willingly sacrifice anything to keep her safe, including his own heart. He would not fail the woman he loved again.

He turned the doorknob and slipped inside. Looks like Lucy had been expecting him. Either that or she was being unforgivably careless. Lucy sat up the moment he entered. No feigning to be asleep, no pretense of surprise when she looked at him. No. His Lucy never wasted her time with such nonsense. She just gave him a slow smile of welcome.

"Come to join me?" Lucy said, allowing the sleeve of her nightdress to slip off her shoulder as she leaned forward.

Finn froze. Her hair hung loose about her face, trailing down her back. The expanse of pale skin that her gown exposed stretched from her long, elegant neck to just below the jointure of her arm and shoulder. The top of one breast swelled dangerously near the neckline. He took a step toward the bed, his body moving toward her of its own volition.

Lucy's smile widened and she shifted just a bit, letting the material slip farther down her arm. Finn closed his eyes and grit his teeth. This isn't what he came here for. He pictured Philip's face, the leer in his eyes that he was careful to conceal from Lucy but that Finn saw every time the man looked at her. Finn needed to focus on why he'd risked coming to Lucy tonight.

He stalked to the end of her bed and Lucy's quick intake of breath nearly made him forget everything. He could still feel her lips against his, could still taste her on his tongue. His heart thumped erratically. For half a second, he warred with himself. But then Finn grasped the robe that was lying across the bottom of her bed and tossed it to her.

"I came to talk. I'll wait until you put that on."

"I'm not cold."

Finn glared at her and Lucy bit her lip, though her smile still peeked through. The nightdress covered her from neck to ankle and down to her wrists. Other than the bit of shoulder that was showing she was fairly well hidden under the mass of fabric. But the material was so thin he could see the hint of her skin beneath it. The knowledge that there was nothing else beneath the gown stirred parts of him that were better left alone.

"Lucy," he said, his voice strained.

"Very well. I'll admit I'm curious as to what you deem so important that you'd risk being seen in my room."

She slipped out of bed and shrugged into the robe. "Better?"

Finn gave her a curt nod, but he didn't relax. With the robe pulled tight across her body and tied at the waist, it merely served to accentuate each delicious curve of her. And it didn't erase the knowledge that there was very little beneath it. Finn's hands itched to touch each and every inch of her, and by the smile on her face, Lucy was well aware of that fact.

She smiled and sauntered over to an armchair by the fireplace. He followed, sitting opposite her.

"So?" she prompted. "You said I didn't understand the danger I was in. Explain it to me."

Finn leaned forward, his elbows resting on his knees. "You know that when I was in Boston, I was involved with a ring of smugglers."

"Yes. But your boss was killed when we got Coraline back. You were free of them."

"No. I'm not free. The organization has a sort of hierarchy. The man your sister killed was merely a manager of sorts."

Lucy paled. "So who is the leader of this organization?"

"Philip Halford."

Lucy sat back, her hand to her chest. Her breath quickened a little, though while she looked upset, she didn't seem particularly surprised.

"How does he manage to run a criminal organization of that size and be such a public figure? Everyone here knows who he is. How does he keep his involvement hidden? More importantly, how in the world did you get mixed up with someone like him?"

Finn sat back. "That's a very long story."

Lucy crossed her legs and folded her arms across her chest. "I've got nothing but time."

She gently bounced the foot of her crossed leg, her lips pursed. Every bounce shifted the robe farther so that her leg was exposed to her calf. Finn swallowed and looked away. The woman was going to be the death of him, she really was.

Talking was his only salvation.

"Before I came to work for your sister, I worked in England."

Lucy nodded. "For that earl or prince or some muckety-muck."

A ghost of a smile crossed Finn's lips. "A duke, yes."

Lucy shook her head. "I find it impossible to envision you in full uniform, serving some titled old bag."

"I served as a butler in your sister's household."

"And you didn't fit in there either. You aren't a man that was born to serve others, Finn."

Finn's jaw clenched and he looked away, not wanting to admit how close to home she'd struck. Jake had found him the job with the duke, who had been living in San Francisco at the time. Finn hadn't been in the position to turn down a well-paying *legal* job and the duke was more than happy to add Finn to the collection of oddities he collected. A butler with tribal tattoos on his face wouldn't be something that anyone else in the duke's circles could claim. Finn had found he was good at the job. He hadn't enjoyed it, per se. As Lucy accurately stated, he wasn't a man made to serve others and taking orders from the crazy old bird had been trying. Still, he'd been sad when the old man passed away.

"Anyhow, when the duke died I quite suddenly found myself without employment. His heirs didn't find a tattooed butler 'appropriate' for their household."

Finn said it without bitterness. He'd grown so used to being ostracized for his facial markings, it didn't bother him anymore. In fact, he felt more uncomfortable hiding them, as he was doing now, then letting them show. But he didn't have a choice on the matter at the moment. Halford wanted Finn with him and that meant the tattoos had to be covered.

"So they dismissed you," Lucy said, frowning.

"Yes. I'd expected it, of course. However, they refused to pay me the wages owed me. And that left me in a bit of a bind. I had some money saved, enough to buy passage back to America. But I wanted to save that if I could. So I found a ship's captain who was willing to give me passage in exchange for working onboard the ship during the journey. Their cook had unexpectedly died and I had a decent hand in the kitchen so the arrangement suited me well."

Lucy smiled in surprise. "You cook?"

"Those pastries you loved in Boston? That was me."

Lucy's grin widened. "That would explain why the one time Brynne requested it after you left, it turned out inedible. That was the last time she asked Mrs. Krause to make them. It never occurred to us that you'd made it."

"I'm glad it made an impression," Finn said, returning her smile.

"So," Lucy said, her smile fading as she brought his attention back to his story, "you became a ship's cook. Was Philip on the ship? Was that how you met?"

"I'm getting to that part. Hush."

Lucy grimaced at him but settled back into her chair and waved at him to continue.

"There was a couple aboard, heading to America to proselytize to the wicked heathens they'd heard roamed the country. They spent most of the voyage annoying anyone they could pin down with their dire predictions for anyone they considered 'ungodly.' I made a point to avoid them. The captain and crew had no issue with my tattoos. I was relatively sure the same couldn't be said for this couple and the last thing I wanted to do was cause problems.

"But it is a long voyage and the ship is only so large. I bumped into the woman one night, knocked her right on her backside. She took one look at my face and set to shrieking like I was the devil himself. Her husband came running, along with several members of their group. They beat me to a pulp before the captain could step in to intervene."

Lucy's eyes narrowed. "I would have thought they'd have been pleased to find you there. Would have given them some preaching practice."

Finn shrugged. "The woman got it into her head that I'd attacked her and they didn't give me a chance to explain what had happened. They kicked up such an uproar about having a murderous heathen aboard that the captain was forced to set me ashore."

"He abandoned you? Of all the cowardly, double-crossing, traitorous things to do!"

Finn's heart warmed at her defense of him. "I really couldn't blame him. They were paying passengers. I was not. Dropping me off lost him nothing but an easily replaced cook, whereas getting rid of them would have meant returning their passage fees. I hold no ill will toward him for his decision."

Lucy snorted and muttered something under her breath about vengeance, yellow-bellied cowards, and a particularly sensitive part of a male's anatomy.

Finn chuckled and shook his head. "Yes, well. The captain, and his balls or lack thereof, was the least of my worries. I only had a little money and I was going to have to use what I had to buy passage on the next ship I could find. But before I could do so, I was set upon by thieves. I woke up in a hospital several days later. All my belongings had been stolen."

"Oh, Finn."

Finn shrugged. "It happened. There wasn't anything I could do to change the situation. No use railing against my fate."

Lucy shook her head, her lips pinched. Then she jumped up, and before he could say anything she'd deposited herself in his lap and wrapped her arms about his neck.

"You may not rail against your fate, but I do. You are a good man, Finnegan Taggart. And you deserve so much better from life."

Finn sat frozen for a moment, certain he should remove her from his lap, but wanting to do nothing more than wrap his arms about her and hold her there forever.

"Stop fighting it," Lucy whispered in his ear. She pressed a kiss to his neck and he was lost.

Lucy moaned when Finn crushed her to him, and the sound spurred him on even while in some corner of his mind a warning bell was clanging. He needed to stop this, now, while he still could. His hands reached for her, but instead of pushing her off, they tangled in her hair, angling her face toward him. She met his lips eagerly, opening to him so he could explore every inch of her mouth. She shifted against him, trying to press as much of her soft flesh as she could against him.

"No," Finn said, dragging his mouth from hers. They both panted in the flickering light of the fire, staring at each other while their heart rates slowly calmed. "Lucy, we can't do this. I need to go."

He stood, gently setting her away from him. His heart broke at the mixture of hurt and anger on her face, but he couldn't do something that they'd both regret. Letting her back into his heart meant drawing her into his world, and that was something he could not do. Not while he worked for Halford. Maybe not ever. He had too many enemies. Too many who would hurt Lucy just to get to him. The image of Rachel bleeding at his feet flashed through his memory and he flinched away from it. The thought of Lucy ending up the same way burned a hole in his heart. He couldn't live if she came to harm because of him.

"You haven't told me what happened," she said, barring his way to the door. "How did you get mixed up with Philip?"

Finn sighed and raked his hand through his hair. "Philip found me in that hospital. He paid for my care, offered to pay for my passage to America."

"And in return?"

"In return, I'd be sort of an indentured servant. I'd work

for him, doing whatever he asked, for a period of time."

Lucy took a long, slow breath. "For how long?"

"Ten years."

"And how many of those years do you have left?"

"A year and a half, give or take. I worked for him a short while before I came to your sister in Boston."

"I'm surprised he let you work for her if you are such an asset to him."

Finn shrugged. "He was against it at first. But as long as it didn't interfere with the duties he laid out for me, he was willing to give me a little leeway. And he thought having me in the household of a wealthy socialite might afford him future opportunities he could cultivate. I would never have exploited Brynne for his gain, but he didn't need to know that."

Lucy snorted. "Sure. You wouldn't exploit her; just kidnap her daughter for ransom."

Anger spiked through him at the reminder. At her for bringing it up and at himself for allowing the situation to happen in the first place. "You know why I did what I did."

Lucy bit her lip and looked down. "I know." She glanced back up at him through her lashes and his heart clenched, any anger he'd felt melting away. God, but she was beautiful.

"I know you were just protecting Coraline. I'm sorry."

He nodded. Her eyes roamed over his face, focusing on his lips for a moment before coming back to meet his gaze.

"Couldn't you…couldn't you just disappear? You and I, we could go someplace, somewhere far away. Australia, maybe. Or back to California, to your family, your tribe…"

"No. I can't ever go back there."

Lucy frowned but Finn wasn't ready to delve into that story. "I appreciate your concern on my behalf, but I don't want you involved. Halford might be a corrupt swine, but he did save my life once. I owe him a debt, and I always pay my debts. Besides, there are always ways around the more disagreeable tasks he sets me. And so far, I haven't done much except follow him around and make sure no one plunges a knife in his back."

"So you'll continue to be at his beck and call for the next two years?"

Finn tried to ignore the sinking feeling that permeated through him when he gazed at Lucy. He'd give anything to run away with her. But she wouldn't be happy if she were never to see her sisters again. And if Halford ever found them, Lucy would be nothing more than a way to punish Finn. He wouldn't allow that to happen to her.

He stood and walked to the door.

"Finn, wait."

He paused with his hand on the knob, his eyes on the ground while he gathered the strength to walk out of the room and leave her there. "I was happy to see you, Lucy," he said quietly. "I'm glad to know that you are okay, that your family is doing well. But I wish you had never come."

He glanced up, steeling himself for the pain he'd see in her face at his words. The pain was there, swimming in her eyes with her unshed tears. But mixed with it was an anger that burned hot and fierce. Good. If he could stoke that anger hot enough, maybe it would burn so brightly it would incinerate the last of the love she felt for him. He dreaded what he was about to do. The bile rose from the pit of his stomach but he choked it down and turned to face her.

It would hurt him less if he could tear out his own heart and hand it to her, but if he had to hurt her to keep her safe, he would. Even if doing so would destroy him in the process.

"Halford might play nice for the public, but he isn't someone to trifle with. Give up this game and go home. You won't win. I don't deny that I desire you. You're a beautiful woman and I've been alone a very long time. But it means nothing more than that. I did love you once, but that was a long time ago. Now, all you are is a liability. A thing from my past that I wish had stayed buried. Go home before you destroy both our lives."

He turned and left her standing there, her tears streaming down her face. The sight would join the other image he had of her, when he'd left her in Boston, both haunting him for the rest of his life. He hurried through the hotel as quickly as he could.

And when he was safe inside his own room, he sank to the floor and let his own tears flow.

Chapter Eight

Lucy stared into the cup of coffee before her. She hadn't slept at all after Finn had left. The ache he left behind each time he touched her was becoming unbearable. And there were too many thoughts running through her mind, too much breaking her heart. She had never felt so bone weary and soul sick in her life. Considering what she had been through in the last several years, that was saying something indeed.

A knock sounded at her door.

"Enter," she called.

"The carriage is ready to take us to the school, miss." Lilah entered and took Lucy's shawl from the armoire.

Lucy stared into her cup a moment longer. If she had any sense of self-preservation, she'd be on the next train to Boston.

"Thank you, Lilah. I'm afraid I won't be able to stay too long. Mr. Halford has invited me to the theater tonight."

A slight purse of the maid's lips was the only indication that she didn't approve.

"What is it, Lilah?"

The maid glanced at the door, as if expecting someone to be there listening and then sat down opposite Lucy. "I know it's not my place, Miz Lucy, but I think it would be best if you didn't see too much of Mr. Halford."

Lucy cocked her head. "And why is that?"

"It's only, well Mr. Halford…he's…well, he's…"

"It's okay, Lilah. Tell me what you know."

"He's not a good man. He pretends to be. But deep down, he's a bad one."

Lucy turned her back so Lilah could drape the shawl across her shoulders. "I know that."

Lilah's mouth dropped open. "Then why do you stay? Why do you keep lettin' him court you? You should get far away from him."

"It's not that simple. I need to help my friend."

"Mr. Taggart?"

A faint smile crossed Lucy's lips. "Yes."

Lilah cocked her head, her eyes narrowed slightly as she scrutinized Lucy. "You still love that man?"

Lucy looked at her maid, surprised at her forwardness. It wasn't that long ago that the woman had been a slave, subject to all manner of horrid punishments for lesser infractions than talking out of place. But Lilah returned her gaze, her strength and intelligence shining from her deep brown eyes.

"Yes, I do. Very much."

"And does he love you?"

Lucy gave a mirthless laugh. "Well, that is the question of the day."

Lilah reached across the table and squeezed Lucy's hand. "What happened since the ball? You tell Miz Lilah what's going on. Maybe I can help you figure it out," she said with a smile.

Lucy looked into Lilah's kind, concerned eyes and shook her head. "I don't even know where to begin."

"I've always found the beginnin' a good place to start."

Lucy laughed and took a deep breath. Then she filled Lilah in on her recent bout with Finn. When she was done, the maid sat back in her chair and shook her head. "Well now, that is a tale indeed. Though it does explain why a man like Mr. Taggart is mixed up with one such as Halford. I'd always wondered. What a pickle."

"To put it mildly." Lucy rubbed her forehead, trying to ease the ache behind her eyes. "For the first time in my life, I'm at a loss as to what I should do. When I was younger, it wouldn't have been a question. I would have marched right into Philip's room and demand he release Finn from his bargain. Or better yet, I'd simply truss Finn up like a Christmas goose and put him on the first ship to Australia or some other far off place where Philip would never find him. With me going along to keep him company, of course."

Lilah smiled. "And now?"

Lucy sighed. "Now I'm older. And…a little wiser. Rushing into an ill-thought-out plan would help no one. And though I hate to do it, I have given Finn's wishes in the matter some consideration. I understand why he wants me out of the way. If our positions were reversed, I'd be doing the same thing."

Lilah thought for a moment, her brow creased. "What is it you truly want?"

"I want to stay and fight for him. Need to fight. I need him. I can't even imagine going back to my old life, knowing he is here. But…I think I must consider the possibility that the fight might be over. How many times must the man tell me he doesn't want me, before I listen?"

"Well, at least one more," Lilah said, smiling.

Lucy laughed. And then groaned. "The thing is, I wholeheartedly believe that he truly doesn't want me here, and even though I understand his reasoning, that knowledge still destroys a small part of me."

"Yes, but that's where the true problem lies, isn't it? In that reasoning of his. What you need to do is listen to your gut. What does it say, deep down in your bones?"

Lucy looked back into her teacup, stared into the creamy, brown liquid until her eyes blurred. "My instinct fairly screams that he still loves me."

Lilah nodded. "Then his rejection of you ain't coming from a lack of love, but from too much of it. He just wants you safe. Can't fault a man for that. Ain't that somethin' worth fighting for? After all, what would you do if you were in his position? Indentured to a criminal who would only see a loved one as leverage to use to his own ends? Who belonged to a family he'd already threatened?"

Lucy met Lilah's gaze. "I'd do the same thing. My damned level best to get him as far away as possible."

Lilah nodded. "So."

"So," Lucy echoed. "I have a choice to make. Abide by Finn's wishes and return to Boston, abandoning him to his fate but keeping myself safe. Or stay, and try to help him, free him from the tangled web he's trapped himself in."

"And maybes you can free him to find a future with you."

"Yes."

"You know what you want to do."

"Yes."

"Then why you hemmin' and hawin'?"

"What are the possible consequences my staying might have for Finn? If Philip ever found out who I really am and what I mean to Finn, we'd both be in even greater danger. Philip has already tried to get his hands on a Richardson once, when he ordered the kidnapping of my niece Coraline. I doubt he'll have any qualms about using me to gain what he wishes from my family. And the last thing I want to do is give him something else to use to bend Finn to his will."

"But what if you do nothin' at all? They's consequences

for everythin'. If you give up now, what happens to your man?"

"If I do nothing…Finn will remain a virtual prisoner for another two years. Or worse. I can't imagine Finn will ever be allowed to just walk away."

Lilah didn't say anything, but sat quietly watching as Lucy came to her decision.

"I can't allow that. Not if I can do something to help him."

Lilah thought for a moment and then nodded, coming to a decision of her own. "Well then. I'll help you."

"You will?"

"If it will git you away from that devil Mr. Halford any faster, yes."

"I appreciate it. I could use all the help I could get. But I don't wish to place you in danger. And I'm not sure what you can do."

"Don't you worry none about me. I can take care of myself. As for what I can do to help you, I used to be a part of Mr. Halford's household," Lilah said, her lips thinning.

A knot of ice settled in Lucy's stomach. "You mean you were once his slave."

Lilah jerked her head in a quick nod. "His late wife brought me with her when she married him. I was in his household 'til the day I was freed. As soon as I was able, I left. But I know his house, I know his servants. If it's information you want, I can help you get it."

"I didn't know that he'd been married."

Lilah's lips puckered in a sad frown. "It was many years ago. She died six months after their marriage. And if you ask me, I think she was glad to go."

Lucy raised her eyebrows and Lilah's eyes flashed with anger.

"Mr. Halford treated his wife worse than the dirt on his shoes. He married her for her money and once he got that she weren't no use to him no more. He'd go whorin' and drinkin' right under her nose and after the first beating he gave her, she didn't complain no more. She done her best to stay outta his way, but I still never seen her without a bruise somewhere. Bad enough to be the devil to other folks, and he had plenty evil to spread around. But to his own wife? Like I said, Mr. Halford is a bad man."

"I agree," Lucy said, nauseated at the life his poor wife must have lived. "If we could expose him, show the public who he really is and the crimes he's committed, he'd be arrested. He'd spend the rest of his life in prison."

Lilah snorted. "I'd prefer he get hanged."

"Well, I'm sure his crimes merit it. But I'll settle for getting Finn away from him and ensuring that we won't be looking over our shoulders for the rest of our lives."

"Then we'll just have to come up with a plan."

Lucy smiled. It was good not to be alone in this fight. "Yes, we will. In the meantime, I've been thinking of a few worthy ways I can spend my time. Sitting around this hotel all day has grown a bit wearisome."

"Oh?"

"I've got a few other plans in mind that I'll need your help with. I hope it's okay with you, but I've hired you away for the time being. While I am here, you'll be working for me."

Lilah grinned. "That suits me just fine, Miz Lucy. Just fine, indeed."

Lucy smiled back at her. She could have used her sisters' expertise, but they were far away and Lucy had no intention of dragging them into this mess. They both had husbands and children now. It was best if the only neck being risked was her own.

• • •

From the moment Lucy walked into the school, she was

enchanted. Lilah had done a wonderful job making the place as homey as possible. The school was housed in a small, ramshackle shed behind the small home Lilah shared with her sister Ruby and Ruby's husband and children. There was no furniture in the school, but the walls and floorboards had been recently whitewashed and they'd been able to find an old chalkboard that had been discarded. It was cracked and had a large chunk missing from one corner, but they made do.

Since the students had no slates to use and paper was too expensive to use for sums and alphabet practice, Lilah had had to get a little creative. She'd made several small boxes that she filled with dirt that the students would write in with small twigs and sticks. It was an ingenious solution and Lilah beamed with pride when Lucy told her so. A small bookshelf at the front of the room held a tiny selection of books, but it was clear the modest library was Lilah's pride and joy.

"I save as much as I can from my wages at the hotel, and there is a lady at the general store who will sell me castoff books when she can spare them. I should have enough to buy another soon."

Lucy swallowed past the sudden lump in her throat. It broke her heart that these people had to scrimp and save for things that she'd always taken for granted. Even in her own days of poverty on her family's ranch, when they'd been in danger of losing everything to her corrupt sheriff half brother, they'd had books to educate themselves. And a community who didn't rise up in arms when they tried to do so.

"You've done an amazing job here, Lilah. Truly."

Lilah smiled shyly and looked around at her school with pride.

Lucy walked around the perimeter of the room. The windows were covered with brightly colored fabric that cheered up the bare room considerably. But when Lucy lifted the material to peek outside, she found the window boarded up. She looked questioningly at Lilah, who shrugged.

"I had real pane glass in when the school first started but someone threw a brick through them the first night. After that I used oilpaper but they threw bricks through those as well. The boards aren't as nice, but they do keep the bricks out," she said with a sense of resigned humor that broke Lucy's heart.

"I'd like to help."

"Any help you'd like to offer will be very much appreciated, miss, I assure you. But…I should warn you. Not everyone here will like you helping us."

"Well, those who don't like it can just kiss a plucked chicken's ass. I'll do what I please."

Lilah burst out in shocked laughter and slapped her hand over her mouth. Two small children, their ragged clothing cleanly pressed, peeked shyly around the door.

"And who do we have here?" Lucy asked, smiling at them.

Lilah waved them in. "Come here you two. These are my nephews. Isaiah and Joshua. Say hello to Miz Lucy," she prompted them.

They both murmured hello but wouldn't let go of Lilah's skirts.

Lucy knelt down and held out her hand. "I'm very pleased to meet you both."

She waited until they got up the nerve to shake her hand, one by one, and then plopped down on the floor next to them, tucking her skirts under her crossed legs.

Their eyes rounded in surprise and she patted the floor beside her. They cautiously sat.

Lucy leaned forward, her elbows on her knees, her chin propped in her hands. "So, boys. I could use your help. Will you help me?"

They looked back and forth between each other and then back at Lucy and nodded.

"Excellent. First of all, what is it that you would most like for your school?"

"Anythin' at all?" little Joshua asked.

"Anything at all. What would it be?"

They looked at each other again, coming to a silent agreement. "Desks," said Joshua. "Like the other school up the road."

"And slates," said Isaiah.

Joshua screwed up his nose. "No, I like my dirt box. It's more fun."

Lucy and Lilah laughed. The boys grinned. They liked this wishing game.

"More books!" Joshua said. "Lilah, she been readin' us *Oliver Twist*. It's awful good."

"It is indeed," Lucy agreed with a grin at Lilah.

"I want more stories like that. Lilah says if I try hard, I can maybe read it by myself someday."

"Well, those all sound like very reasonable requests."

"Miss?" Isaiah tugged on her sleeve.

"Yes, Isaiah?"

"If we could wish for anythin', anythin' in the world, I'd want my daddy to be able to come to school, too."

The lump was back in Lucy's throat and she looked up at Lilah.

"Isaiah's daddy Sam works late in the evenings. He could come in the mornin's but he don't want to take up room that the children need."

"Ah. That sounds like a very noble wish, Isaiah. I'll see what I can do."

"Really, miss?"

"Really," Lucy promised.

"All right, you two." Lilah bustled them up and shooed them out the door. "Miz Lucy needs to be getting back and you two need to go help your mama."

"'Bye, Miss Lucy!" they called as they ran out the door.

Lucy laughed and waved back. She gathered up her shawl and followed Lilah back to the carriage, settling inside with a renewed sense of spirit and purpose.

She didn't know what was going to happen with Finn. She prayed he'd come around eventually. But she was done wallowing alone in her hotel room while she waited for him to see reason. Plans for a new schoolhouse were already flowing through her mind. It felt good to have a worthy cause to fight for again. She was going to build those kids the best schoolhouse they had ever seen, and she'd make sure their parents were able to benefit from it as well.

Lucy was so excited she could scarcely hold still, running through a checklist in her mind of all she needed to do.

"As soon as we get to the hotel, I need to wire my sisters and our bank manager. Once we get the money squared away, we need to find some property I can purchase where we can build the new school. I can build a little house on the property as well. That will be much easier than living in the hotel. It'll be nice to have my own space again. And once we get the building underway we'll need to find the supplies we need. Perhaps we can build benches for the students instead of individual desks. The backs of the benches can have small desks built into the backs of them, for the children to write on. That will probably be easier than separate desks. I'm sure there is someone in town who can build those. And then…"

Lucy trailed off, finally catching sight of Lilah's downturned face. "What is it, Lilah? Oh dear," she said, a thought just occurring to her. "I'm overstepping, aren't I? I'm so sorry. I didn't mean to. This is your school and you've done a wonderful job with it. I didn't mean to come in and start making plans for changing everything without even asking you.

"Oh no, Miz Lucy! That's not it at all. I think your plans are wonderful. Heaven sent! Truly. It's only…"

"What?"

Lilah pursed her lips. "There's a lot of folks 'round here that won't be happy with what you got planned."

Lucy frowned. "I've already told you what I think of those people."

Lilah gave her a faint smile, but pressed on. "The thing is, it's one thing for you to help out at our school. Some folks would have been aggrieved enough at that. But what you talkin' about, building a school for us...well some folks are going to be fit to be tied, no doubt about it. I'm sure your family won't want you mixed up in somethin' like this. People down here...they don't like change. And jus because some law says they have to treat folks differently, don't mean they listen. I just don't want you to have to deal with..."

"The things you deal with every day?" Lucy asked with a wry smile.

Lilah gave a short laugh. "Yes."

Lucy leaned forward and took Lilah's hand. "First of all, my family will be behind me one hundred percent. It's sort of a family tradition to take on monumental and unpopular tasks. And secondly, I'm stronger than I look and I don't give a riled-up skunk's hind end about anyone's opinion of what I do with my time and money. I'll spend both as I see fit and anyone who has a problem with that can—"

"I know. I know. They can go kiss a plucked chicken's ass."

Both women laughed and Lilah settled back looking much relieved.

Lucy, however, despite what she said, felt the first qualm of unease break through her excitement. She'd dealt with bigoted, prejudiced people before. But she knew the situation here was unlike anything she'd ever encountered before. The South may have lost the war, but there were many who weren't taking the loss quietly.

Well, Lucy had never backed down from a fight in her life. She wasn't about to start now.

Chapter Nine

Thanks to her sisters and a very helpful bank manager, Lucy had the perfect property picked out and purchased within a week. It was amazing what one could accomplish with a ready supply of cash. In short order, Lucy had hired a crew of men Lilah found who were already erecting the walls at both the schoolhouse and the little cottage she was having built for herself on the back of the property.

She stood surveying the construction of her cottage, happiness warming her along with the sun that shone down on the little clearing. The property was picturesque. All green and lush with life, with a little creek that flowed between the clearings where her house and the school would sit. She'd had a little bridge built over the creek and already had visions of children scampering across the lawn on their way to school.

It was wonderful to have a purpose again, to have a real plan for what to do with her life. And to have a place to call her own. She'd done okay in Boston, working with Brynne and Richard at the clinic. But that was their dream, their home. Lucy wanted one of her own.

A touch of sadness invaded her excitement. Her dream would never be complete without Finn. She still held out hope that he'd find a way out from under Philip's thumb. But until he did, she was happy to have something worthwhile she could do with her life.

A horse cantered to a stop behind her and she didn't need to turn around to know who it was. It was as if her thoughts had summoned him. He dismounted and came up behind her, close enough that she could feel his presence, though far enough away that no part of him touched her. If she reached her hand out, she could feel him. Instead, she clenched them into fists around the folds of her skirts.

"What can I do for you, Mr. Taggart?"

"This is madness, Lucy. What are you doing?"

"I should think it's quite obvious."

Finn released an exasperated breath. "Why do you have to be so stubborn?"

The frustration in his voice brought a smile to her lips. Poor man. Dealing with a Richardson when she'd made up her mind was enough to drive the most patient man insane. She almost felt sorry for him. Almost.

"I'm sorry that you do not approve, Finn. But as you are not my husband, or even my lover," she said, turning to pin him with her gaze, "and you have made it quite clear you desire to be neither, you really have no say in what I do with my life."

He grabbed her arms and pulled her closer, though he stopped just shy of bringing her against his chest.

The only part of him that touched her were his gloved hands, but that was enough. She could feel the heat of him burning into her flesh. And unless she were very much mistaken, the sudden hunger in his eyes meant he could feel it, too. He released her and Lucy had to bite her tongue to keep from crying out.

"A lot of folks around here aren't happy about this school of yours," he said.

"I have no interest whatsoever in what these bigoted tyrants think. Lilah's students have every right to get an education and if their community isn't willing to provide them with one, I certainly have the time, money, and desire to do so."

"Bad things happen to those who rock the boat here."

Lucy pulled herself from his grasp. "I can't believe I'm hearing this from you, of all people. I'm not some coward who goes running scared because a few overindulged, arrogant prats want to keep living their deluded lives. The war is over. They lost. They need to start getting used to the new way the world works."

"That's what you aren't understanding. The war never ended for a lot of these people. They aren't happy about the changes that are being made and they have a nasty habit of retaliating against those who don't agree with them. I just want you to be safe."

Lucy waved him off. "I'll be perfectly fine. It's just a school, for heaven's sake. What harm is there in teaching people to read and write?"

"To most people, nothing. And I'm sure there are some in the community who admire what you are doing here. It's those who don't that I'm worried about."

"Oh, what can they do? Let the old windbags stand on their stoops and bluster about. What harm can they do?"

"More than you can imagine. I mean it, Lucy. This isn't a game."

"You keep telling me that, like I'm a child who doesn't understand what you're saying. I know that there will be some who won't like this. But as long as I stay out of their way, I don't see why they'd get in mine. The school is on my private property, and like it or not, I have every right to build it, so they can complain all they'd like. I'm not playing any game, Finn. I came here to find you, yes. And I haven't given up on us. But I have no desire to sit in the hotel, biding my time until you get it through your thick head that we belong together.

"You wanted me to move on with my life? Well, I've moved on. I've stayed away from you as you requested. This has nothing to do with you. I've found something worthwhile to do with my time. People I can help. And nothing you say is going to make me change my mind about it."

Finn's eyes darted around the clearing, taking in the schoolhouse, and Lucy's small cottage, with a growing expression that Lucy could only describe as panic. What was wrong with the man?

"What if I agreed to leave with you? Tonight? Would you go?"

Lucy sucked in her breath, her heart pounding so fiercely she thought it might jump from her chest. It was her greatest wish. She wanted to be with him more than anything. But did he truly mean it? She searched his face, looking for some sign that he might be insincere. But his face was carefully blank, except for the intensity of his gaze.

Then a cheer went up as the last wall of the schoolhouse was hammered into place. Lucy looked over Finn's shoulder at Isaiah and Joshua who were jumping up and down, huge grins spread on their faces.

"I...I can't just leave...I promised..."

"You don't need to be here to see the completion. The school is nearly built. You could leave enough to supply it, run it. Leave Lilah in charge. Come away with me."

Lucy slapped her arms against her sides in exasperation. "Why, Finn? Why now? I've been trying to get you to leave ever since I came here and you've refused, broken my heart over and over again, told me that you didn't want me here. And now that I've found a purpose for my sorry life, found something I can find joy in *without* you, you want me to just abandon it? I can't do that! I can't just walk away from this, from these people."

A few of the builders stopped and looked at them curiously. Finn grabbed Lucy's hand and towed her into the trees until they were out of sight of prying eyes.

"I thought you wanted this. Isn't this what you've been begging me for since you came?"

Lucy took a deep breath through her nose, trying to keep her composure. "Yes, it's what I wanted, but you aren't doing it for the right reason."

Finn threw his hands up. "You can't be serious! I'm trying to give you what you want and now you're changing your mind."

"I'm not changing my mind."

"But you just said—"

"I said you were doing it for the wrong reason. Yes, I want us to be together, any way that is possible. And if that meant running away together, then so be it. But I don't want that if the only reason you are doing it is out of some misguided sense of chivalry. I don't want to be having this same conversation in some remote destination the next time something dangerous happens. I don't want you running off with me just because you think it'll keep me safe. I want you to want to be with me because you love me."

Lucy heard the pleading note in her voice and she hated it. But it just felt too cruel to be offered what she wanted most at the expense of someone else's well-being. She couldn't just abandon Lilah and her students now. She couldn't let them down, not when she promised she'd help them. And besides, what Finn offered her wasn't really what she wanted either. It was like being handed a piece of fool's gold and being told it was real. It might look pretty and even dupe those who should know better, but it was still just a worthless rock. Lucy wanted better. They both deserved better.

"Do you love me, Finn? Do you want to run off with me because you can't stand to be away from me anymore? Or are you just saying anything to get me to leave town? Because if it's the latter, then—"

Finn's mouth descended, effectively cutting off anything she'd been about to say. She thought for a split second about pushing him away, and then he grasped her chin and angled her head up, giving him better access to her lips. A small moan escaped Lucy's throat and Finn surged against her, pressing her back against a tree, imprisoning her body while he ravished her mouth.

"Miz Lucy! Miz Lucy!"

Lilah's voice rang through the clearing and Finn raised his head, his breath coming in heated pants that mingled with her own. She had his lapels crushed in her fists and she forced herself to let him go. Lilah's footsteps grew nearer and Lucy pushed away from the tree, reaching up to pat her hair and brush the twigs and leaves from her clothing.

"Miz Lucy?"

"Here, Lilah," Lucy called, resolutely keeping her gaze from Finn as she left the shelter of the trees.

"Oh, Miz Lucy, there you are." The maid's shrewd gaze looked back and forth between Finn and Lucy, but she didn't say anything about finding them hiding in the shadows.

"What is it, Lilah?"

"Mr. Halford's carriage just pulled up. He's lookin' for you."

"Thank you, Lilah. I'm coming."

The maid nodded and hurried back toward the schoolhouse where Philip stood waiting. Lucy went to follow but Finn grabbed her hand.

"We'll talk about this later."

"There's nothing to talk about, Finn. I can't leave just yet, not when we've just started."

"Lucy…"

Lucy shook her head. "You say you want to leave to keep me safe. Well I want to stay to keep you safe. If we run now, we'll always be running. I want to be with you, I really do. But I don't want to be looking over our shoulders for our whole lives. If you are ready to talk about a plan to get you free of him, let me know. I want a future with you. One that doesn't involve Philip hunting you down."

Finn's eyes bore into hers, but he didn't say anything.

Lucy gently pulled her hand from his grasp. "If you'll excuse me, my school has its first visitor."

She walked away, praying she was doing the right thing. Lucy glanced back at her little cottage, at Finn standing in the clearing, watching her with longing in his eyes. Her happily ever after. But if she wanted the fairy tale, she would have to get rid of the wicked king first.

• • •

Finn watched her walk away, toward Halford. The urge to grab her and run was so great he had to close his eyes to shut out the sight. It didn't help that she was right. Leaving now would remove them from immediate danger, but they'd always be looking over their shoulders, always waiting for their pasts to catch up to them. He wanted better for her, better for them.

Which meant he needed to find a way to get Halford removed from the picture. A difficult task. If he could just kill the man, their problems would be solved. Finn didn't feel the slightest qualm at the grim thought. The man deserved to die for the crimes he had committed, that he continued to commit. And Finn would do worse than murder to keep Lucy safe. The problem, well, one of them, aside from whatever lingering moral guilt that might worm its way into his heart, was that

Halford was a well-known and well-respected member of society. His disappearance wouldn't go unnoticed.

Finn frowned, watching Lucy escort Philip around the work site. She kept her distance from him, subtly pulling from his grasp when he'd reach to take her elbow or place a hand on her back. At least she had taken his warning about the man seriously. But she couldn't help the excited animation in her face as she pointed out the features the schoolhouse would boast. She was pleased with her project, and had every right to be. Finn was immensely proud of her, and impressed at the strength of her character in the face of the opposition she must know she faced from the community.

What made him frown was the look on Halford's face when Lucy wasn't looking. The sneer of disgust when he looked at the workers, at the children. The very people Lucy intended to teach. When Lucy faced him, he was careful to show only polite interest.

Lucy caught his eye and sent him a look that let him know she was very well aware of Halford's true feelings. That gave him some comfort. But not much.

No, if Finn wanted his freedom from Halford, he'd have to reveal the man for who he really was. A lecherous, black-hearted, corrupt piece of filth that didn't deserve to walk down the same street as respectable folk, let alone be elected to lead them.

The other problem was that Halford was a master in covering his tracks. He might hold all the strings, but he had hundreds of puppets doing his bidding. And he was very, very good at making sure none of those strings led back to him. In fact, a great many of them would lead back to Finn himself. So any attempt to bring down Halford could effectively take Finn down as well.

Finn was willing to make the sacrifice if there was no other way to keep Lucy safe. But if he could find a way to get rid of Halford and leave himself free to be with Lucy, he wanted to find it.

In the meantime, he'd keep watch over her as he'd done since the moment she'd arrived back in his life. And he'd pray to the God he wasn't sure he believed in to keep her safe.

Chapter Ten

The school hadn't even been open for a day when the first incident occurred. Lucy had welcomed all the children who could attend bright and early. Many worked and couldn't attend, but Lucy hoped they'd come at night with their parents. Finn had agreed to keep coming at night to help teach. Lucy assumed they'd have a larger crowd in the evenings, once work and chores were done.

The first morning, Lucy had been thrilled to find twenty students on the school's steps. Mostly children, but a handful of the mothers wished to stay as well. Lucy welcomed them inside, her heart near to bursting as they took in the large schoolroom, set up with its rows of benches, large chalkboard set up in the front, a desk for Lucy, and even some pictures and maps that Lucy had found to adorn the walls.

Her new students entered eagerly and sat in their places, reverently touching the slates and new pieces of chalk in their special holders on the backs of the benches. The absolute best part of the morning was when Isaiah and Joshua walked in, holding the hand of their father. He shyly took a seat in the back of the room, Isaiah beaming next to him on the bench. Joshua ran over to the brand-new bookshelf that sat between two large windows. He ran a hesitant finger along the spines of the books that filled the shelves.

"Are these for us, miss?"

Lucy had to swallow a few times before she could speak past the lump in her throat. "They sure are."

His smile was so wide the rest of his face almost disappeared. Lucy turned her back and dabbed at her eyes and then took her place at the front of the room. They spent a very productive morning going over some of the basics of the three R's and Lucy was delighted to find that many of her students had at least a cursory knowledge of how to read and write. They were all bright and eager to learn, which made her job easy. A few of the adults left after an hour or so, but most of her students were able to stay until she released them at noon.

Lucy went about straightening the room, putting books back on the shelf, erasing the chalkboard, and getting everything ready for that evening's classes. She'd just walked past one of the windows when something crashed through it, shattering one of the panes. Lucy jumped, her hand pressed to her racing heart, and turned to see what it was.

A brick, with the word *hore* scratched onto it. Lucy hurried to the window and looked out, hoping she could catch who'd done it. A few horses were riding away, but they were too far for Lucy to make out who they were.

Lucy glared down at the brick in her hand. "Ignorant jackasses. The least they could do is spell it right."

Lilah rushed in. "Miz Lucy, you okay?" She took in the broken window and the brick in Lucy's hand and shook her head, her lips pursed in resigned anger. "I told you, miss. Folks 'round these parts ain't too happy with what you doing here."

Lucy placed the brick on the bookcase and went to the

small closet at the back of the room for a broom and dustpan. "They don't have to be happy about it," she said, sweeping up the glass. "I have every right to do as I please on my own property, and if I catch them on it again, I'll make sure they know that I won't stand for their harassment. They should be ashamed of themselves!"

Lilah gave her a sad smile, tinged with pity that sent a fresh rush of anger through Lucy. Not directed at Lilah, but at the people who put that look on her face. That look that said that she'd dealt with much worse and would do so again because that was just her lot in life. Lucy swept the glass into the dustpan that Lilah held for her, even more determined to make her school a success. She wouldn't let those cowards win.

. . .

When Finn walked into the school, he immediately saw the broken pane of glass. Lucy's stony face left no opening for questions, but Finn caught her eye, his brow raised. She nodded at him, gave him a small smile. She was okay. For now. But he was not. The incidents would get worse, he knew.

He hated it when he was right.

Over the next few weeks, small incidents continued to occur. Rocks through the windows. Filthy words painted on the side of the schoolhouse. Once, someone broke down the door and spread manure all over the benches. The worse the situation became, the closer of an eye Finn tried to keep on her. Lucy didn't make this easy. She refused his help nearly every time he offered. She wouldn't let him accompany her to the market, though even that simple task had taken on a sinister tone. The shop owner who'd once treated Lucy with kindness and respect now barely looked her in the eye, slamming her purchases onto the counter with barely concealed contempt.

It was all Finn could do to keep from marching into the shop and throttling the man. Along with everyone else who uttered snide comments or turned hateful gazes her way.

A few acquaintances remained friendly, but not one commended her for what she was doing. Not one offered to help. And not one person defended her from the malicious remarks more and more people aimed in her direction.

Yet each time something happened, Finn saw Lucy's resolve strengthen, her determination to make the school a success, and make the community accept it, grow stronger. She walked down the streets with her head held high, insisting on fighting her own fights, and refusing to allow him to retaliate in any way. She did her best to ignore the cruel treatment that grew more hateful by the day and she showed up to teach each morning with renewed energy and vigor. By God, the woman amazed him. She was extraordinary, pure and simple. But she was human, and he knew the continuous harassment was wearing on her.

One night he entered the school to find that the window had yet again been broken. Lucy had stubbornly replaced each window that had been shattered, but if this kept up, there wouldn't be any glass left in all of North Carolina. After the last incident, Finn had installed sturdy shutters over the windows, but those apparently hadn't helped. The hooligans had just darted in during the dark of night, broken the shutters into kindling, and then went to work on the windows. Finn also worried that after a time these simple scare tactics wouldn't be enough for the perpetrators. Soon, they might decide that more drastic measures were necessary. Lucy still pigheadedly believed that they would back down once they saw she wasn't going anywhere. Finn knew better. And he was terrified for her. It was happening again. The woman he loved was in danger and his failure to save her from it gnawed at him like a starving beast.

He didn't mention it until the last of their students had left for the night. By the time he'd said good night to the last student and closed the schoolhouse door, his emotions were at a boiling point. Lilah looked back and forth between the two of them and slipped out the door with a hurried wave of good-bye.

Lucy grabbed the broom and set herself to sweeping the floor though there was hardly a speck on it. Finn watched her for a moment but she resolutely kept her gaze on her task. The silence stretched so thick between them he could scarcely breathe. When he could stand it no more, he marched to her and grasped the broom.

She glanced at him then, just long enough to shoot him a glare that should have incinerated him on the spot. Then she let go of the broom and tried to walk away, but Finn grabbed her arm.

"I don't want to talk about it, Finn. It was just a stupid prank."

"How many times has this happened now? They aren't going to stop, Lucy. And next time—"

"You don't know that there will be a next ti—"

Glass splintered and fiery droplets rained down on them as a wine bottle with a lit rag sailed over their heads and crashed into one of the benches behind them. The liquid in the shattered bottle splattered, igniting the bench and floor.

"No!" Lucy screamed. She ripped the curtains down from the window and began beating at the fire. Finn did the same, smothering the flames until they went out, leaving the bench and floor charred.

Finn ran for the door, but whoever had thrown the bottle had fled. "Miserable little cowards," he muttered, adrenaline coursing through his system so fiercely his heart was about to jump from his chest. He searched the tree line, watching for any sign of movement, but there was none. The clearing was dark and silent and Finn was suddenly acutely aware of how alone he and Lucy were.

He wished she'd stayed in the hotel, surrounded by people, where he could look after her. They weren't far from town; she'd wanted to be close enough that her students wouldn't have any difficulty getting to her. But they were far enough away that no one would hear her scream if she needed help.

He went back inside, determined to talk some sense into her, but the sight of her stopped him short. She'd grabbed a bucket and scrub brush and was trying to clean the charred surface of the bench and floor. She plunged a blistered hand into the bucket and then went back to scrubbing, ignoring the tears that streamed down her face.

"Lucy," he said, quietly sinking down beside her. She stopped scrubbing but she didn't look up.

"Lucy," he said again, reaching over to take the brush from her hands.

"No." She jerked away from him and went back to scrubbing. "I don't want them to see this. When they come tomorrow. I don't want them to know."

He reached over again and grabbed the brush before she could jerk it away. "Let me."

She looked up at him, the sorrow in her eyes breaking his heart.

"I'll do it. You rest a moment."

She waited until he started scrubbing before she slumped back against a bench, staring at the floor, though he didn't think she saw it. Her hands lay carefully in her lap. He stopped scrubbing and gently took her hand in his, his gut clenching at the blisters on her skin.

"Just a moment," he said, going to her desk and grabbing the vase of flowers she'd set there. He took it into the yard, dumped it, and refilled it with clean, cool water from the pump near the door. When he brought it back in, Lucy was still sitting staring at the floor but she'd stopped crying. He took that as a good sign.

Finn set the vase next to her and eased her hand into the water. Lucy let out a sigh and closed her eyes.

"Thank you," she murmured.

He understood why she wanted to keep the incident from the students, and he even agreed with it. But he hated to see her there, hurt and disheartened. However, he knew her well enough to know she wouldn't let him focus on her until the task was done, so he set about putting the room to rights as quickly as he could. The leftover whitewash sat in the closet and he pulled that out and touched up the scorch marks and made sure all the broken glass was swept up and disposed of.

As soon as everything was touched up and readied for the next day, Finn knelt beside Lucy. She hadn't said a word while he'd gone about cleaning up. It worried him. Lucy was *never* at a loss for words. He cupped her cheek, turning her face until she looked at him.

"Why are they doing this?" she asked quietly. "We aren't harming anyone here. Why do they care if a bunch of former slaves can read and write? What possible difference does it make to them?"

Finn shook his head. "I wish I could tell you, love. I suspect it's easier to not say anything, to look the other way. Or to go along with those who make the loudest noise. That's why good people like you are needed in the world."

Finn smiled down at Lucy, warmth spreading through him when she returned it with a small one of her own.

"Come on, lass. Let's get you to bed."

Finn stood and pulled Lucy to her feet, then swept her into his arms, ignoring her squeaked protest.

"Hush. None of that. Just let me take care of you for once, will you?"

Lucy's forehead crinkled as she looked at him, as if he

were a puzzle she couldn't quite figure out. But she relaxed in his arms and allowed him to carry her to her little house behind the school.

By the time he'd gotten to her front door, he was huffing and puffing a little more than he cared to admit. The bright side was that it brought a smile to Lucy's face, albeit a small one.

"Are your muscles failing you, Mr. Taggart?" she asked, one corner of her mouth turned up in a saucy grin.

"Ock, my muscles are as brawny as always. Perhaps you've put on a few pounds since last I saw you."

Lucy gasped and slapped at him with her good hand, but a bit of her usual twinkle had returned to her eyes.

She helpfully unlatched the door for him and he entered, kicking it closed behind him. He looked around, having never been in her home. He could tell immediately who dwelled there. The room had a small sitting area on one side, an overstuffed chair pulled close to the fireplace and a small sofa angled to catch both the warmth of the hearth and the eye of whomever sat before the fire. A dining table, chairs, and the kitchen took up the rest of the space.

All was clean and tidy, homey but uncluttered, decorated in shades of yellows, browns, and reds. Organized to the point of obsession, with everything in its proper place, yet the space was inviting and welcoming, like Lucy was herself.

He could picture himself in this home. Sitting before the fire in that big chair, Lucy bustling about in the kitchen. Or better yet, settled in his lap, her fingers twining in his hair, tilting her head up for his kiss.

Finn cleared his throat, trying to erase the image from his mind. Now wasn't the time. Not yet. Not until he was free.

"Bedroom?"

"In the back," Lucy said, pointing to a door off the kitchen he hadn't noticed.

Finn carried her into her room and placed her on the large four-poster bed. Lucy sank into her pillows with a grateful sigh and Finn turned to fill the blue-and-white china basin from its matching ewer. He carried it carefully to the bed and Lucy sank her hand into it without prompting from him.

Her breath hissed out and she closed her eyes.

"We need to put something on that. Have you any salve?"

Lucy shook her head and Finn frowned at her.

"Stop frowning at me," she said, though she hadn't opened her eyes.

"Know me that well, do you?"

She cracked open one lid and peeked at him. "Yes, I do. Now don't go busting my britches. I haven't lived here long and I spend most of my time at the school. I haven't had the chance to stock all the necessaries just yet. Lilah will have some. She's just down the lane a ways."

Finn stood. "I'll go and fetch some."

Lucy grabbed his hand before he could leave. "Wait. Don't go just yet."

All playfulness had left her voice, leaving her sounding young and scared.

"I won't be gone long, I promise. But we need to get something on that hand."

"I know."

But she didn't let go. Her thumb rubbed across his knuckles in slow, even strokes and a kick of heat hit him in the lower gut.

"Lucy…"

"Don't go, Finn. Please. Stay with me."

Finn hesitated. He knew it wasn't a good idea. Even after the night they'd been through, all he could think about was that they were alone, in her bedroom. And he wanted to do much more than comfort her.

But one look in those deep brown eyes of hers and he

was lost. He took the bowl of water away, soaked a cloth, and gently wrapped her hand and then settled back beside her with a sigh, putting his arm about her. She snuggled into his chest, hanging onto his shirt with her good hand as though she were afraid if she didn't keep a good grip on him, he'd flee.

"They're going to keep coming back, aren't they?" she asked.

Finn's arm tightened about her. "Yes. I think they will."

"It's all so senseless! What harm is there in educating them? It's not hurting anyone. It's not changing anything that hasn't already been changed."

Finn wrapped his arms around Lucy and pulled her back into his embrace, rocking her, stroking her hair. "I know, love. I know. I've watched it since before the war. And it hasn't changed much since then. I think it will be a very long time before things do change."

He kissed the top of her head, her forehead, tilted her head up and kissed her nose. "But it's people like you that will help make that change happen. Good, kind, strong people who are willing to stand up for what's right."

"It doesn't feel like enough."

Finn kissed her gently, his heart swelling with pride for the amazing woman he held. "You amaze me, do you know that?"

He kissed her again, his lips lingering longer. The tension slowly melted out of Lucy and her lips opened beneath his. Finn groaned, his tongue plunging into the heat of her mouth, his hand slipping into her hair. Lucy wrapped her arm around his shoulders. She slipped farther down the pillows, pulling him with her until he leaned over her.

He knew he should stop this. Letting this get out of hand would only hurt Lucy more, and he'd vowed to keep that from happening.

Lucy's tongue darted out and met his. Her hand fisted in

his shirt and she pulled him closer with a little sigh.

That sound was his undoing. Finn stretched out beside her, nudging his leg between hers so he could lay half on top of her. Lucy was busy trying to unbutton his shirt with one good hand while he was equally busy trying to unbutton the high-necked collar of her bodice. Their breathing echoed in the quiet room and Finn's heart pounded so fiercely he thought it might burst.

He dragged his lips away from hers so he could taste her throat, his lips trailing to the small bit of flesh he'd exposed.

A knock at the front door paralyzed him. Finn and Lucy stared at one another for a second and then there was another knock.

They sat up, hurriedly putting each other to rights. Finn slid off the bed and went to see who it was.

"Miz Lucy?" He could hear Lilah calling through the door. "Miz Lucy, you there?"

Finn opened the door.

Lilah stared up at him, her mouth hanging open. "Oh. Mr. Taggart. I…I didn't expect to see you…"

"Lucy is in the back. She's injured her hand and is resting."

Lilah's mouth snapped shut, her eyes flashing fury. "I heard that ruckus, all them boys leaving. Hoped nothin' had happened, that they were just out pitchin' a fit like usual. I checked the schoolhouse. You all did a good job cleaning up whatever happened, but it's clear something went on there tonight. Is Miz Lucy okay?"

"Yes, come on in. She's burned her hand, but it isn't too bad. It could use some salve though."

Lilah smiled and patted the basket hanging on her arm. "I thought I'd best bring this along just in case. I know Miz Lucy ain't got much here and I thought if anythin' had happened, she might be needin' a bit of something."

Finn smiled at the woman, pleased that Lucy had someone

like Lilah looking after her.

"Just go on back. I know she'll be glad to see you."

"Ain't you coming?"

"No, I...I better be going. If you could make my excuses..."

"Nuh-uh, no sir. I've got enough excuses of my own. If you goin' to be slippin' out the back door like a thief in the night, you can just go along and make your own excuses."

Lilah stared him down, her hands on her hips, until Finn smiled. "You're right, of course. I'll just go, uh, make those excuses then."

"That's more like it," Lilah said, planting herself on the sofa. "I'll just wait here 'til you're done."

"That's not necessary..."

But Lilah just waved him off. "Go on now."

Finn chuckled and went back into the bedroom.

Lucy was up, tidying her hair. "Was that Lilah I heard?"

"Yes," Finn said, standing in the doorway. He was afraid if he got too close, he'd throw her on the bed and finish what they had started, Lilah or no Lilah. And he was running out of excuses to keep from doing just that.

Lucy smiled at him and his heart kicked up a few beats. Oh yes. He'd just have to work harder to get out from under Halford's thumb. Because staying away from Lucy was becoming intolerable.

"I must go," he told her.

Lucy came closer, wrapped her arms about his waist, and rose up on tiptoe to kiss him. He hesitated only a second before leaning down to meet her lips. The sweet taste of her on his tongue nearly drove him to folly. He wanted nothing more than to crush her to him, mark her as his in every way possible. Instead, he gently eased from her embrace and stepped away.

"I won't be able to come to the school for a few days. Halford has me playing errand boy again. Can you stay out of trouble for that long?"

Lucy snorted. "I'll do what I can, but I'm not making any promises."

Finn forced a laugh though he found it far from funny. "Well, I suppose that will have to do."

He gave her a little bow and turned to go.

"Finn."

He looked back at her.

"You stay out of trouble, too."

He thought about making a funny quip, but her face was deadly serious.

He nodded. "I will. I'll see you soon, Lucy."

"Until then."

She gave him a small smile and he turned and left her standing alone.

Chapter Eleven

Lucy's hope that the persecution would stop grew over the next two weeks. There hadn't been another incident since the night of the firebomb. Perhaps the miscreants had finally realized that she wasn't going anywhere and had given up. A small thread of worry always stayed with her, but as each day passed peacefully, Lucy began to think the struggle might be over.

A far greater worry in her mind was Finn. She hadn't seen him since that night. Lilah had brought word from the hotel that he hadn't been back, so he must still be on whatever mission Philip had sent him on, and the thought of what he might be doing frightened her.

She and Lilah were nearly finished straightening the schoolhouse for the night, but Lucy had no desire to go back to her little cottage all alone. If she had to spend one more evening with nothing to do but worry about Finn, she'd go mad.

"Well, looks like we're about finished here," she said, sounding more disappointed that their work was done than she should be.

"My sister's got a big pot of fish stew boilin', if you'd care to join us for supper. I know it's probably nothin' like what you're used to but you're welcome to it."

Lucy smiled, gratitude at the woman's kindness and intuition flowing through her. "I've fought off coyotes for a pail of burned beans. Believe me, I'm used to some pretty awful things."

Lilah's mouth dropped open and Lucy laughed. "Oh, Lilah dear, I could tell you some stories. I wasn't always as fortunate as I am now."

"I'd like to hear some of those stories," Lilah said, grinning at her.

"Well, I'd be honored to join you for supper. And perhaps afterward, I'll regale you with the sordid tales of my past."

The women walked out the door laughing, Lucy's heart lighter than it had been since Finn left.

They spent a very pleasant evening with Lilah's family. Lucy's belly was pleasantly stuffed with the most delicious stew she'd ever eaten and she was lounging lazily by the fire in their small house when Isaiah bounced over to her.

"Miz Lucy, tell us a story!"

"Yes. Maybe one of them sordid tales you mentioned," Lilah said, smiling.

Lucy laughed. "Hmm, well let's see." She racked her brain for something she could tell them that would be appropriate for children's ears. She had had quite a few adventures in her bandit days. Perhaps she should just tell them the beginning.

"Once upon a time," she said, giving Lilah a little wink, "there were three sisters who lived in a beautiful place called California. They lived on a ranch with their mother and father who loved them very much. Sadly, their parents died. But they weren't all alone. They had two very loyal servants named Carmen and Miguel who stayed to help the sisters.

"But their half brother was the sheriff of their small town, and he was an evil, greedy man. He wanted to take the ranch from the sisters because he thought there was a gold mine on the property. He also loved power, and he ran the town with an iron fist. The sheriff terrorized the townspeople and taxed them beyond their endurance."

"Oh no," Joshua gasped. "What did the sisters do?"

Isaiah shushed him and Lucy smiled. "The sisters were very young. But knew they had to do something to protect their ranch, and their town, from the evil sheriff. So the middle sister, Cilla, came up with a plan. They would just have to steal back all the money that the evil sheriff had taken from the people. They would have to disguise their identities. So they started a story about a bandit named Blood Blade, who roamed the trails raiding unsuspecting stagecoaches and travelers. But the bandits never harmed the innocent townspeople. They only stole from the evil sheriff and his henchmen. And everything they took, they gave back to the townspeople. They helped them with food and supplies also, leaving gifts for the people who were in need of help."

"Did they ever get caught?" Joshua asked.

"One of the sisters was caught once, but the others were able to free her. And after years of fighting the evil sheriff, they finally defeated him for good and found a good man to be the new sheriff."

"Did they all live happily ever after?"

Lucy's smile faded a bit. "Almost. Two of the bandit sisters got their happily ever afters. One is still searching for hers."

"Will she get it?" Isaiah asked.

"I hope so," Lucy said, forcing her smile back. She glanced at Lilah, only to find the other woman staring out the window.

"What is it, Lilah?"

Lilah started and looked at Lucy. "Oh, prob'ly nothing. I just thought..." She glanced at the children.

"Never mind for now. You two," she said to the kids, "off

to bed with you. Tell Miz Lucy thank you for the story."

The boys jumped up, gave Lucy hugs along with their thanks, and scampered off to bed. Lucy went to join Lilah by the window.

"What is it?" she asked again.

"Look at the sky." Lilah pointed west, up the lane a bit where the schoolhouse and Lucy's cottage sat. The sun had set and the sky was dark, but there seemed to be a faint glow still. Lilah pushed the window open and the evening breeze brought the distinct smell of smoke.

"The school!" Lucy tore from the house, running toward the schoolhouse, Lilah close on her heels.

They closer they got to the school, the brighter the glow became. The stench of smoke grew thicker and Lucy ran harder, her heart in her throat. She already knew what she'd find when they rounded the bend onto her property. But she held out hope until the last second that she'd be wrong.

Lucy skidded to a halt in the school courtyard. Because what she saw was far worse than anything she'd imagined. The school itself was fine. It sat in its clearing, untouched. But in the small courtyard in front of it stood a cross, the flames that engulfed it throwing menacing shadows on the whitewashed walls of the school…and on the semicircle of white linen clad men.

There were ten of them, seated on their horses, their faces completely covered by white hoods, with nothing but two eyeholes cut into them. The horses pawed the ground, snorting their dislike at being so close to the burning cross. Lucy didn't blame them. The sight sickened her. Her head swam with the force of the hate she felt for the cowards before her. The so-called men who were so terrified of change that they had to terrorize two unprotected women.

"Who are you?" Lucy called out, reaching an arm out to keep Lilah behind her. She began edging toward the school's door.

"They're Klan," Lilah whispered, the terror in her voice igniting a deep burning fury in Lucy's gut.

"Who are you?" she asked again, almost screaming the words. "You have no right to be here. This is *my* property and I'm telling you all to leave. Now!"

"It's you who have no right to be here, you damn Yankee bitch," one of the men said, though Lucy had no idea which.

"This is my property," Lucy said again. "You are trespassing."

"They won't listen," Lilah whispered, tugging on Lucy's arm. They were close to the schoolhouse door now.

"What you are doing here is an abomination," shouted another man.

They'd reached the bottom step that led into the school. The horses were tossing their heads, shifting and pawing at the dirt, picking up on their riders growing agitation.

"You're a traitor to your own kind!" yelled another.

"Get inside," Lucy said to Lilah, shoving her up the stairs.

"You can't hide! Those walls won't protect you! We are here to bring you to justice!"

Lucy stumbled after Lilah, slamming the door shut behind her. She leaned against it for half a second, trying to get her furiously beating heart under control. Lilah sank onto a bench, her tear-filled eyes wild as the men's hateful shouts from outside carried to them through the broken windows of the school.

Lucy pushed away from the door and marched to the closet.

"What are you doing?" Lilah asked as Lucy wrenched the door open and stood on tiptoe, reaching her arm back as far as she could onto the shelf inside.

Lucy pulled out a shotgun and then reached up again for the ammunition. "I'm not letting anyone terrorize me on my own property. Let alone a bunch of cowards running around in their night sheets."

Lucy loaded the gun and marched to the window, ripping down the new curtains she'd recently hung to cover the broken windows.

"Lucy, no!"

But Lucy already had the gun aimed through one of the broken panes. "Don't worry," she assured the other woman. "That story I told your nephews wasn't just a fanciful bedtime story. I could shoot the rattle off a snake from a much farther distance than this. I can certainly shoot the hood off a yellow-bellied weasel or two."

Lucy yelled out the window. "I'm giving you until the count of three to get off my property, or I'll be forced to defend myself!"

A smattering of laughter let her know what they thought of her threats. Lucy smiled. It was so much fun when an enemy underestimated her.

"One!"

The horses shifted a bit, the men looking back and forth at each other. None of them pulled a weapon. Lucy doubted anyone had even brought one. Men, especially egotistical and arrogant men like those contaminating her yard, rarely expected a fight from those they considered weaker or inferior to themselves.

"Two!"

"I think she might mean it, Jed."

"No names!" another one hissed. His words were quiet but Lucy's blood ran cold. She knew that voice.

She focused on him. On his build, the way he sat his horse, his expertise at handling his animal.

"Why that insufferable, miserable, piece of week-old horse shit!" Lucy cursed under her breath.

She aimed the gun at the man she very much suspected

was none other than Philip Halford himself.

"Three!"

The men didn't move. Lucy took a deep breath, blew it out, aimed carefully, and pulled the trigger.

The gun fired and the man she thought was Philip yelled. She'd only grazed him. While she'd dearly love to shoot him right there in her yard, doing so might not be a good idea. Just yet anyway.

"Shit, she's really shooting!" one of them shouted.

Lucy fired again, this time hitting the ground near the feet of one of their horses. The horse reared, throwing the rider off, and then took off at a dead run. The rider, who hastily pulled his hood back into place, took off after it.

Lucy yelled through the window as she loaded new shells into the gun's chamber. "Those were warning shots. Next time I won't miss!"

A few more horses rode off and by the time Lucy had the gun loaded and ready to fire again, only one horse and rider stood in the courtyard. He looked toward the schoolhouse for a moment and then turned and rode off.

Lucy watched out the window, waiting to see if any of them would come back. And wondering if that had indeed been Philip under that hood. Whoever it was had been the man who'd stayed behind to give her that parting look to make sure she knew he wasn't afraid of her.

But none of them came back.

The adrenaline that had been coursing through her system started wearing off, and Lucy carefully lowered the rifle with suddenly shaking hands. She took a tremulous step away from the window and Lilah hurried forward to take the gun from her. Lucy stumbled to a bench and sank down, her hand pressed to her pounding heart.

More shouts echoed from the courtyard and Lucy jumped to her feet, but Lilah grabbed her arm.

"It's just Sam."

Lilah ran to the door to let Sam and the others with him know she and Lucy were all right. The men started a line from the water pump, filling a bucket up and passing it down until they had the cross doused. They had the smoldering timbers pulled down in record time. But Lucy knew the image would always be seared into her mind.

Once Sam and his friends had cleaned up the sacrilegious mess as best they could, and made sure that Lucy was okay, they returned to their homes. Lilah saw Lucy to her little cottage. Lucy stood on the threshold, looking around at the home that only a few hours before had felt like such a refuge, and realized that despite her anger and her bravado, she didn't want to be alone there.

"Lilah," she said quietly.

"I was wonderin' if you'd mind if I stayed with you tonight," Lilah said. Lucy looked at her and Lilah smiled. "What just happened is enough to shake anyone, I reckon. I think we'll both sleep a might better if we weren't alone."

"I'd be very grateful, Lilah. Thank you."

"My pleasure, Miz Lucy."

Lilah started a small fire in the hearth while Lucy found a few quilts and made up a bed for her friend on the sofa.

"I think Philip was there," she said, finally voicing the thought that wouldn't leave her mind.

"It wouldn't surprise me," Lilah answered.

Lucy frowned. "Really?" She thought for a moment. "I suppose it doesn't surprise me that he'd want to be part of something like that. But it does surprise me that he'd follow through on it. For a man who needs to keep a large majority of his affairs private, it seems like an unnecessary risk to be involved with such a group."

Lilah shrugged. "Seems to me like he's just the sort of man who'd fit right in with them."

Lucy thought for a moment longer. "No matter what the sentiments of those down here, being involved in such activities wouldn't be the best for Philip politically if they were known. He's certainly committed crimes while he thought he was hiding in his bedsheets. Maybe if we could find proof that he was part of this tonight, or that he was part of similar incidents, it would be enough to bring him down. Maybe even get him arrested. And once one crime is known, others are sure to be exposed."

"The only place to find proof would be at his home. He won't keep anythin' that will tie him to the Klan where just anyone can find it."

"Well then, we'll just have to search his house." Lucy smiled at the horrified look on Lilah's face.

"Why do you want to jump right into the lion's den?"

"It's the best place to look. The sooner we get him exposed for the evil, corrupt coward that he is, the better for our students and our school…and Finn."

Lilah chewed that over for a minute and finally nodded. "So, how do we get into his house?"

"That won't be a problem. I've already been invited to his annual Fall Social at the end of the week. The trouble will be bringing you with me."

"Oh, that's no trouble. I take it you've never heard of the Halford's Fall Socials."

Lucy shook her head.

"It's an all-day affair. Guests will begin arrivin' soon after breakfast. There will be croquet on the lawn and some other games and after lunch, the ladies will retire to rest for the afternoon so they can be fresh for the ball that evening. All the ladies will be bringing their maids to help them dress for the evenin.'"

"Excellent. Well then, I suppose we have nothing to do now but wait."

Chapter Twelve

Well, Lucy would give one thing to Philip. The man knew how to throw a party. Groups of gaily dressed people milled around the lawn of Philip's estate, chatting, munching on delicious hors d'oeuvres, and generally having a wonderful time. A few months ago, Lucy would have been included. Now, aside from a few polite nods in her direction and one or two brave souls who'd deigned to speak to her, most people steered clear. Everyone had heard what had happened at her school, and those who had once been content to look the other way had, for the most part, decided they were safer avoiding her company. No one wanted to risk being drawn into her fight. She could understand that, but she condemned it all the same.

Finn stepped out of the house and on to the veranda, his gaze scanning the crowd on the lawn beneath him. All thoughts of her nighttime visitors disappeared as she stared up at him. Her breath caught in her throat and her stomach did a little flip. It didn't matter how much time she spent in his company, seeing him again, even after such a short time, always made her feel like a twitterpated schoolgirl.

Lucy knew the moment Finn caught site of her. His bland, polite expression changed to one of surprise and then irritation. He accepted a drink from a passing servant and casually made his way across the lawn to her side. He stood facing away from her but so close their shoulders touched. He didn't look at her, his gaze continuously scanning the yard, but his words were said so only she could hear them.

"What are you doing here?"

"I was invited."

Finn shot her an exasperated look and she buried her grin in her punch cup. Her smile faded as she glanced around, took in the groups of her acquaintances that were, for the most part, studiously avoiding her company. She sighed and leaned closer to Finn, letting the full length of her shoulder and arm press against him.

"How long have you been back?"

"I've only just returned."

Lucy nodded. That would explain why he hadn't mentioned her little incident. Well…he'd hear about it sooner than later so he might as well hear it from her.

"I had a little visit from a group of sheeted-up men. They burned a cross in my yard, threatened me and Lilah."

Finn stiffened and looked at her with an intensity that made her take a step back.

"Are you all right?"

A lump rose in Lucy's throat and she dropped her gaze. She'd been able to hold it together all this time, but a simple question from him and she was ready to fall into his arms blubbering. It was beyond maddening. She cleared her throat. "I'm fine. I shot a few warning shots at them and they scattered like the cowards they are."

Finn snorted and shook his head. "You never cease to surprise me, Lucy."

Lucy cocked an eyebrow. "I'm not sure if that's a

compliment or not." She gave him a small smile. "In any case, to answer your earlier question, I'm fairly sure that Philip was one of my masked intruders that night."

Finn turned his gaze back to the room, but she could see his jaw clenching. "What makes you think that?"

"I know his voice."

Finn was silent for a moment. "Well. If he is involved in any nocturnal activities, it's not something he's ever shared with me. Though I wouldn't be surprised. But that makes your presence here even less advisable, so I'll repeat, what are you doing here?"

Lucy glared at him. "I'm going to find some proof that Philip is the lying, conniving, bedsheet-wearing snake that I know him to be and expose him once and for all. I'm going to find something, anything, that will provide the evidence that will free us both from him." She looked back at the crowd. "And I can't very well do that from home now, can I?"

"Don't do this, Lucy. Go home. We can discuss this later. I will help you if I can. But for now, go home, lay low. If the Klan has already paid you a visit, it is only going to get worse. I know you love your school, but…"

"Don't say it, Finn. I'm not going to let a bunch of cowards, who won't even show their faces, run me out of town."

Before Finn could speak again, Lucy caught sight of Lilah toward the veranda of the house. "Now, if you'll excuse me…"

"Lucy…"

But Lucy ignored him. It warmed her heart that he was concerned, but she wasn't going to let him dissuade her from her course of action. Philip had terrorized those she cared about for far too long. She would do everything she could to bring him down.

Lucy's impatience grew with each girlish twitter from the other women in the room. The single women had been given a suite of rooms in which to refresh themselves before the ball that evening and there were ladies in various states of dishevelment all over the place. Several were napping on the large bed and chaise lounges that were spread through the rooms. Others were excitedly exclaiming over each other's ball gowns, while their maids scurried to and fro trying to keep their mistresses' belongings in order.

Finally, Lilah stuck her head in and nodded. Lucy followed her out, calling over her shoulder that she was going out for some air when a few of the ladies questioned where she was headed.

As soon as the door closed behind them, Lucy took a deep breath. Her nerves were a jumble of chaos, and the incessant chatter had driven her to the brink of madness.

She followed Lilah down the long hallway toward the back stairs. "Mr. Halford has organized a ride for his male guests. We should have plenty of time to search his office before they return."

Lilah led her down the stairs, through the bustling kitchen, and out into the main floor of the house. Lilah didn't slow down but marched purposefully toward a closed door. Lucy followed behind, acting for all the world as if she'd just been summoned and had every right to be heading toward Mr. Halford's private office.

When they reached the door, Lilah glanced quickly around and then pulled a key out of her bodice. Lucy's eyebrows raised, but she said nothing until they were safely inside the office.

"Do I want to know how you got the key?" Lucy asked.

Lilah smirked. "I still have friends here. It was easy enough to take if off the housekeeper while her attention was on the fine bottle of brandy I brung her. And no, you don't want to know where I got that."

Lucy smiled and shook her head, then got to work exploring the room while Lilah kept a lookout at the door. The office was filled with wall-to-wall bookcases that were stacked with books and small knickknacks. She did a quick perusal of the shelves on her way to the enormous desk set between two floor-to-ceiling windows at the far end of the room. She doubted Philip would leave anything incriminating out in the open where anyone could see.

She tried the drawers on the desks but they were all locked. No matter. She'd come prepared for that. Lucy had yet to come across a lock she couldn't pick, much to her sisters' envy. She knelt on the floor, her skirts billowing around her, and yanked two pins from her hair. She quickly bent them to the shape she needed to help hold the lock's internal pins out of the way and got to work.

The lock to the largest drawer clicked and Lucy triumphantly pulled it out. Inside were rows of files. She glanced through each one, but none seemed to be out of the ordinary. Household inventories, campaign documents, travel records. Nothing of any importance. Nothing that shouted I'm a corrupt criminal, come lock me up.

Lilah squeaked and closed the door, locking it, seconds before Philip's voice boomed through the entryway beyond the door.

"He's back!" Lilah ran toward a bookcase near the door, shoving on a section of it to reveal a small, hidden closet and beckoned to Lucy to follow her.

Lucy slammed the drawer shut and ran for the closet. She made it inside just as the door to the office opened and Philip entered.

"I thought you said he was gone," hissed Lucy.

"I thought he was. The rest of the gentlemen left. He should have gone with them."

"Shh." Lucy put her finger to her lips and strained to hear through the door.

He was speaking to someone, though it took Lucy a moment to realize who it was.

Finn.

Lucy pressed her ear to the thin wood wall, struggling to hear what they were saying. Their voices were muffled, but she could make out most of what they were saying.

. . .

Finn glanced around Philip's office, certain he'd heard something as they were entering. Everything looked in order but he couldn't shake the feeling that something was off. He half expected to see Lucy's skirts sticking out from beneath the desk. He wouldn't put it past her to break into Philip's office. But Philip took a seat at his desk without incident, so for now, it seemed, Lucy must be minding her manners.

However, Finn was in no way fooled that her restraint would last. He could almost see the fury bubbling under her surface whenever he looked at her. And to be honest, he couldn't blame her. Halford was threatening her school and those Lucy held dear. She wouldn't let it continue for much longer. One of these days, something she couldn't ignore would happen and she'd retaliate.

Knowing Lucy and her penchant for playing the martyred hero, he feared he knew exactly what that might be. Instead of heeding his warning about Halford and leaving town, she'd probably taken it upon herself to try and free Finn from Halford's grasp. The thought made Finn's blood boil with anger and fear…and a healthy dose of pride, if he were honest.

He couldn't help admiring her spunk and was touched that she'd risk so much on his behalf. But the tender feelings ended there. The blasted woman was going to get them both killed: her because Halford would never let her get away with whatever she was planning, and him because he'd die before he let Halford harm one beautiful inch of her.

Halford unlocked his top desk drawer and handed Finn a sheaf of papers. "I need you to go to the docks tonight. I have some cargo coming in and you must supervise the unloading."

"Is it something one of the other men can handle?"

"Under normal circumstances, possibly. But tonight's shipment contains a few special items that won't be listed on the inventory sheet. I need you to oversee it personally."

Finn hesitated and Halford cocked an eyebrow. "Is there a problem?"

"No. Of course not."

"I know you've just returned, but it's only one more night. I need my best man on this one."

"Of course." Finn forced a smile, though his gut was churning. He hadn't seen Lucy in far too long and the need to assure himself of her well-being was becoming overwhelming.

"Did you have other plans?" Halford's voice was cold. Finn wasn't doing as good of a job hiding his emotions as he used to.

"Not really, no. I'd thought to perhaps stop in and make sure Lucy was settling in to her new home. I don't want to shirk my familial duties."

Halford turned away, hiding his expression, and Finn's suspicions were immediately raised.

"Don't worry about your cousin. I'll make sure she's taken care of."

Finn's blood ran cold.

"Oh come now. Surely you trust me with her."

"Trust you with a beautiful woman?" Finn said, trying to inject as much good-natured male humor into his voice as he could. It was difficult when all he wanted to do was wrap his hands around Philip's throat.

Philip let out a hearty laugh. "Don't worry, Taggart. I'll treat her with the same care and consideration as you will show the special cargo you'll be handling. That way we can both be assured that our respective treasures are safe. It would be tragic if either of them were to fall into the wrong hands."

Finn didn't miss the warning in Halford's voice. The man was too shrewd. If Finn had had any thought of double-crossing him, letting his cargo fall into the hands of the authorities, it was gone now. And the thought had crossed his mind a time or two. If Philip were to be arrested, his whole corrupt empire would disintegrate and Finn would be free. Philip didn't trust anyone enough to share his power. Finn was the closest thing he had to a right-hand man. The rest of Philip's network was flunkies and thugs that Philip hired while he kept tight hold of the reins.

But with Halford essentially holding Lucy hostage, Finn's continued loyalty was assured. Which was the exact situation Finn had been trying to avoid when he'd attempted to make Lucy leave. Stubborn woman.

"Will we have any problems tonight?" Philip asked.

Finn met his gaze and did his best to keep his fury contained. He knew his face was devoid of expression. He'd had years to practice keeping his emotions hidden. But he didn't think Philip was fooled.

"No. No problems."

"Good. Then I'll expect you back with the special shipment by early morning. The rest of the cargo you can send on to the warehouses."

"Yes, sir."

"Now, if you'll excuse me, I must go entertain my guests."

Finn inclined his head and watched Philip leave the room. He needed to find Lucy. He'd get her on the next train to Boston if he had to hog-tie her and shove her in a gunnysack to do it. Finn stormed out of the office. The time for cajoling and threatening was over.

Chapter Thirteen

The gentle breeze through the trees would have been peaceful under normal circumstances. But at the moment, the mist that seemed to hang over everything, mixed with the pungent scent of horse and unwashed male, only served to intensify the churning of Lucy's belly. She and Lilah watched Finn from the shadows of a building amid a row of warehouses, Lilah hunkering further into her cloak as a cold breeze blew through the alleyways.

It was a dark night. The men were scarcely visible, though every now and then Lucy caught sight of Finn's face in the light of the lanterns. Lucy slid down and leaned against the wall of the building, trying to make herself comfortable while they waited for something to happen. Lilah followed suit but had a much harder time of it as she tried to tuck her skirts about her legs.

That was one of the many reasons that Lucy, much to Lilah's horror, had raided the laundry at Philip's house and was wearing one of his suits along with a coat she'd found hanging in a spare closet. If it was one thing Lucy had learned from her bandit days, it was to dress appropriately for every situation. A spying expedition to the warehouse district in the middle of the night, along with wherever Finn would be moving the cargo, called for attire that would allow her to move uninhibited.

So far, nothing too exciting had happened. Finn stood near the wagons with a checklist, checking each box that was unloaded. Lucy hadn't seen any cargo that looked in any way suspicious and other than the men that were unloading the crates, Finn hadn't spoken to anyone else. Whatever this special shipment of Philip's was, it either hadn't been unloaded yet or was secreted within the regular cargo.

"Nothing's happening," Lilah whispered, stamping her feet a bit to warm them up.

Lucy leaned forward, craning her neck around the corner of the building, and took another look before ducking back. "It looks like they are almost done unloading. Come on," she said, pulling Lilah up. "We need to be ready to move."

Finn had been directing where each crate went as it came off the wagons. The vast majority of the crates had been loaded into the warehouse that Lucy assumed belonged to Philip. But a small number of crates had been loaded onto a separate wagon. While each of the other wagons was accompanied by a driver and one other man, this wagon had four men. That must be the one with the special cargo.

Lucy watched while Finn finished up with the man in charge of the shipment and marched over to the overly guarded wagon. He jumped up beside the driver and they were off.

"Let's go," Lucy said, hurrying over to where her horse sat waiting.

Lilah's face puckered, but she gamely clambered onto the horse behind Lucy. Lucy had learned that Lilah hated horses and hadn't been too pleased to find they'd be riding one. But it was much easier to quietly follow someone on a single horse than it would have been in a carriage. Lucy would have preferred to go on foot, but she had no idea how far they'd be traveling and she wanted a means of quick escape if it became necessary.

She kept her distance from the wagon, ensuring her horse was hidden within the trees that lined the road. If Finn had been alone, she wouldn't have worried so much. But the four thugs accompanying him were bad news, and if Lucy could avoid a confrontation with them, she would. Especially with Lilah clinging to her back. Lucy could handle herself, but she didn't want to put her friend in any more danger than she already had.

They followed the wagon for some time before Lucy became aware that they were nearing Philip's property. After a few more minutes, the wagon stopped at a dilapidated gate that marked the boundary of the property. Finn hopped down and opened it and waved the wagon through. Lucy waited until the wagon had rumbled around the bend in the road and then rode up to the fence line and climbed off the horse.

"We'll have to go on foot from here," she told Lilah as she helped her down.

"What about the horse?"

"We'll leave her tied up here. I don't think they'll be going far. They'll keep the cargo out of sight of the house, so there must be a place at the back of the property where they are going to unload the cargo."

Lilah froze, her whole body going rigid. "The old slave quarters are back here."

"Does anyone use them anymore?"

Lilah shook her head. "Folks think they're haunted, won't go near them. There was a bad fire there during the war. Most of them burned down. Killed several slaves."

The pain in Lilah's voice tore at Lucy's heart. "Oh, Lilah,

I'm so sorry."

"Weren't your fault," she said with her good old Southern logic. "Mr. Halford never bothered to clear them out and since he no longer runs his cotton plantation, he don't have need of 'em. The house servants have rooms in the attics."

"Well, it sounds like the perfect place for hiding secret cargo."

"I reckon it is. Maybe it's better if we wait a spell though. There's no sense in us bustin' in there with all them men hangin' around. It'd be safer for sure if we wait 'til they all leave."

"Perhaps, but we can't know for certain where they are taking the cargo or even if it's really illegal. If we are going to defeat Philip, we need solid evidence, and we aren't going to find that hiding out in our bedrooms. We need to see what they have and where they are putting it."

Lilah took a deep breath and blew it out. "All right, then. Let's go."

Lucy took her by the hand and led the way through the trees and brush, following the trail the wagon had taken. After several minutes, a group of shacks came into view. The structures were arranged in a large half circle, like a small village surrounding a communal square. All of the buildings showed signs of the fire. Some were nothing but piles of burned timber and rubble. Others had been gutted by the flames, though the walls, or some of them, had been left standing. Only two were still in relatively decent condition, though they had also been scorched.

It was into one of these that Finn's men had unloaded the crates from the wagon. By the time Lucy and Lilah crouched down behind the back wall, the wagon stood empty in front of the shack. Lucy carefully peeked through the remains of a window. Finn stood near the door of the structure, apparently giving instructions to three of the men. They all nodded at whatever he said and then he turned and left. He either had a horse waiting that they hadn't seen or had taken one of the wagon horses because a few moments later, Lucy heard the distinct sound of hooves riding away.

She looked around the interior one last time. The remnants of the previous occupants were still there. A broken table and a couple chairs sat in one corner. Various piles of rubble and unidentifiable bits of household items were scattered here and there. The crates, however, were nowhere to be seen. And neither was the fourth man.

A shiver of unease crawled up Lucy's spine. She grabbed Lilah's hand to run. But when they turned to flee, they came face-to-face with the missing thug…and his gun, which was aimed right at their heads.

"Evenin'," he said.

Lucy slowly raised her hands, but Lilah gasped and opened her mouth to scream.

The man cocked the gun. "None of that now, ya hear?"

Lilah's mouth snapped shut with a whimper, but she nodded her head.

"Come on." He gestured with the gun, directing them around to the front of the shack.

Lucy's mind raced. Finn had left but he couldn't have gone too far. If she screamed, he might hear her. But then what? Lucy hated the thread of distrust that wormed its way into her consciousness, but she had to admit that she wasn't one hundred percent positive that Finn would get her out of this situation. Or that he *could* get her out of it even if he wanted to. These were Philip's men. They might take orders from Finn, but Lucy couldn't count on their loyalty to him.

Even if she could, she had been caught spying on them. She knew the secret cargo was hidden somewhere nearby. Finn might be forced to do something he might not want to do. Even with her at his back, they were outnumbered. Lucy didn't count the trembling maid at her side. The last thing she wanted to do was get Lilah hurt.

They were nearing the corner of the building. Around that corner, the other three men waited. If Lucy was going to act, she needed to do it now.

She put her arm around Lilah, acting as though she were comforting the maid. She leaned in as close as she could and whispered, "When I tell you to run, go! Get to the horse as fast as you can and get out of here."

Before Lilah could respond, Lucy shoved her to the ground and rounded on the man with the gun. She ducked and barreled into him, her shoulder connecting with his gut. Her momentum knocked him off his feet and made his shot go wide.

"Go!" Lucy shouted to Lilah.

Lilah hesitated only a second, but when she heard the shouts of the other men, she took off like a flash, disappearing into the trees.

Lucy grappled with the man on the ground. He'd dropped his gun somewhere, but he had a firm hold on her waist. She reared back as far as she could and slammed her elbow into his nose. He bellowed but he let go.

Lucy sprinted away but was knocked flat when one of the other men launched himself at her, tackling her to the ground. She struggled against his hold, but he had the upper hand. He sat on her, his legs straddled on each side of her thighs keeping her from getting to her feet while he fought to pin her arms to the ground. It didn't take long. No matter how much fight she had in her, the man outweighed her by a good hundred or more pounds.

During their fight, her hat had fallen away, leaving her braid tumbling down her shoulders.

The man looked down at her, panting heavily in her face. She could tell the instant he finally registered that she was female. The fury in his eyes transformed into a smug anticipation and the ball of revulsion in her gut churned with a fresh spike of fear.

"Well now. Looky what we've got here."

He stood, hauling her up with him, keeping his beefy hand firmly gripped around her wrists. He wrenched her arms behind her back and marched her past the two men who'd been watching their fight. The third man glared daggers at her, his hand clamped to his bleeding nose. She winked at him. She didn't know what possessed her, but she couldn't help herself. He roared and stumbled toward her but one of the other men kicked at him.

"Leave off, Jimmy. You'll get your shot at her. We need to have us a little talk first."

Lucy instantly regretted the winking. But damn it all, she was tired of pigheaded men thinking they could do whatever they wanted to her without suffering any consequences.

The men marched her into the shack. One grabbed one of the chairs from the corner and another removed his belt and pulled a handkerchief from his pocket. He tied her hands behind her with the cloth and then made quick work of binding her to the chair with the belt. When she was secure, the one who seemed to be in charge squatted down in front of her.

"Now then. What's a pretty little thing like you doing roaming around at this time of night?"

Lucy shrugged as best she could through the belt binding her arms to the chair. "I couldn't sleep. Thought I'd go for a little walk."

"Humph." He drew his finger down the front of her shirt, his eyes following the trail before glancing back up to meet her gaze. "That's an interesting choice of clothing for a lady."

Lucy repressed her shudder of revulsion. "I didn't want to ruin any of my dresses."

The man dragged his hand down her thigh and stopped midway. He leaned forward, squeezing hard enough that Lucy bit her lip to keep from crying out. "Why don't you just quit the games and tell me what you're really doing out here."

Lucy took a shuddering breath. "I told you, I just wanted some a—"

His hand cracked across her face so hard her head snapped back. She tasted blood, but she couldn't tell if it was coming from her nose or lip.

Fine. They didn't want to play nice. She had no problem with that.

"Do I need to ask you again, or are you ready to talk now?"

"There's only one thing I want to say to you," she said quietly.

"And what's that?" He leaned in again, matching her quiet tone.

"I don't want the others to hear."

He leaned in closer. "Don't want them to hear what?"

"Go to hell," she whispered. Then she reared her head back and head-butted him as hard as she could.

The sight of him falling off his chair as his head snapped back on his neck blacked out for a second and bright spots peppered her vision. He grabbed his head and shook it like a dog and then lurched off the floor at her. She brought her knees up against her chest and before he could stop his momentum, she slammed her feet into his gut and kicked off with every ounce of strength she had.

He went flying backward, shaking the entire building when he hit the wall. Another man charged her and she stood as best she could, swinging the chair she was attached to around to crash into him. The bottom of the chair, already flimsy and damaged from the fire, broke off, though her arms were still tied to the top half. At least she could move her legs freely.

The other two men advanced on her. Lucy's head throbbed and her arms had gone numb from being tied. She staggered back as they came forward. She couldn't fight them both off. She was rapidly losing steam. They flanked her, one coming on each side. Then one lunged. She dodged him, but swerving out of his range put her too close to the other man. He grabbed her from behind, grasping the edges of the chair back she was still tied to.

The other man sneered, hauled back his fist, and slammed it into her face. Lucy dropped to her knees, her head swimming.

"Get back up, bitch!" he shouted, kicking her in the gut.

Lucy groaned and crumpled. It was over. She couldn't fight them both off. And the third man was rising from where he'd been slumped against the wall. Lucy lay on the floor, her face in a rapidly spreading pool of her own blood, and she waited for them to come at her again.

The man she'd kicked against the wall staggered over. He stood staring down at her, his split lip pulling up in a vicious sneer. "You're going to regret that, bitch."

He took off his belt and Lucy swallowed down the bile that threatened to choke her.

"I already do regret it," she said, forcing more bravado into her voice than she really felt.

"Oh yeah?"

"Yeah. I'll never get your putrid stink off my boots."

The man's face twisted in fury and he brought the belt down, the heavy buckle cracking against her hipbone as the leather of the belt seared into her thighs. Lucy cried out and the man smiled, pursed his lips, and spit on her.

"I haven't even gotten started yet, you whore. You're going to be begging me to kill you by the time I'm done with you."

"I don't know, Zeke. A flighty little piece like her, dressing up all indecent and flauntin' herself in those britches. She might just like it. If she don't like you, I'm bettin' she'll be happy to try me on for size."

They laughed. Lucy closed her eyes against the tears that were building. She wouldn't let them see her cry.

At first, the sound of the gunshot didn't register. But when the man holding the belt dropped to the floor, his lifeless eyes staring into hers, she realized she hadn't dreamed it.

Another shot rang out. Another man fell.

The other two scrambled, one searching the ground for a weapon. The other didn't bother but ran for one of the burned out windows. He didn't make it. A third shot echoed through the room and he dropped.

The fourth man lunged for Lucy, trying to drag her in front of him to use as a shield. Lucy went completely limp, forcing the man to hold her dead weight in his sweaty grip. The second she felt his grip slipping, she wrenched around, breaking his hold. She dropped to the ground and scrambled away from him as best she could.

A fourth shot rang out.

And then it was silent but for Lucy's labored breathing and a woman's horrified gasps. Lucy's nose still bled, though it had swollen so much the fluid could barely trickle through the blocked passageways. Her head ached so much she could barely lift it and her arms felt like tiny knives were stabbing her all over.

She glanced up and met Finn's gaze. For a moment, it felt like time stopped. Her entire world reduced down to him. There was no sound but that of her heart beating, no sight of anything but his face. His beautiful, wonderful face that looked upon her with such anguish she felt her own heart shatter.

Finn sank down to his knees and gently peeled back the hair that stuck to the blood on her face. He didn't speak, his jaw clenched so tightly she could see the joint popping in and out near his temple. His breath came in short bursts and Lucy had the feeling that if he could, he'd be howling his fury aloud. She knew the feeling.

Finn pulled his knife from his boot and carefully turned her so he could cut the belt from her arms. She hissed as the blood rushed back into her limbs in a river of fire that lapped at her arms and hands. Finn bent to scoop her into his arms. She couldn't help him at all; her arms were totally useless. He murmured in her ear, soothing words she couldn't understand. She didn't need to. He was there. His heart beat steadily beneath her ear. That's all she needed to hear.

His horse stood waiting outside the door and Finn gently eased her into the saddle. The world tilted for a moment but she hung on as best she could until he climbed up behind her and she was able to settle back against him. He leaned over and took the reins from Lilah, leading the horse she'd clambered up on, then turned their horses back toward town.

"What about them?" Lucy said. She didn't particularly care what came of the men they left behind, but Finn had just killed four men. She didn't want that to come back to hurt him.

"Leave them," Lilah said. "Ain't nobody come here no more. They's enough ghosts to keep dem company here."

"Don't worry about it," Finn said, pressing several kisses into her hair and along her forehead. "Don't give them another thought. Just rest now. I've got you."

Rest. Nothing sounded better.

Lucy slumped against Finn and closed her eyes.

Chapter Fourteen

Lucy drifted in and out over the next several days, but Finn was always there when she opened her eyes. One morning, Lucy woke to find Finn stretched out beside her in the bed, sound asleep. She carefully turned on her side so she could watch him. Her body was still sore, but she felt much better. After gingerly pressing the sore flesh of her face, she determined that the swelling had greatly reduced, though she was sure she looked a fright.

Finn, on the other hand, looked absolutely mouthwatering. He hadn't covered his tattoos since he'd brought her home. There had been no need as he hadn't left her side. She reveled in being able to stare at him, the real him, unimpeded. His mouth parted slightly and his breath moved in and out, making a slight squeaking sound on the exhale. Lucy put her face in her pillow and giggled.

Finn snorted and opened his eyes, looking around the room a moment before his gaze rested on her.

"Good morning," he said, stretching a bit before he turned on his side to face her. "What's so funny?"

Lucy smiled up at him. "You squeak when you sleep."

"I do not."

"Yes, you do. It's the most adorable thing I've ever heard."

Finn gasped with fake offense. "Madam, a man may be many things. Fierce, strong, ferocious, powerful, devastatingly handsome, perhaps. But never adorable."

"Sorry, you are definitely adorable."

He narrowed his eyes and growled. Lucy laughed and then sucked in her breath as the movement jarred her healing face. All merriment dropped from Finn and he reached out a gentle finger to trail along her lip and up her bruised cheek.

"I'm so sorry I didn't get there sooner."

"Shh." Lucy shook her head. "You have nothing to apologize for. Ever."

He caressed her cheek, his eyes creasing in worry and sorrow. Lucy kissed him, cutting off whatever else he might have said.

"You saved me, Finn. That's all that matters. You saved me."

He took a deep, shuddering breath and rested his forehead against hers. They stayed that way for several moments, relishing being in each other's arms. He finally pulled away to look at her again.

"How are you feeling today?"

"Much better," she murmured, enjoying the brush of his hand along her skin. "Really," she said when his eyes narrowed. "I'm still a little sore but I don't feel as stiff and my face doesn't ache as much as it did."

He frowned. "I'm not sure I believe that."

"Why not?"

"Well, I mean no offense by this, but you look like hell."

Lucy laughed again. "I'm sore. But I'll survive. I'm sure it looks worse than it feels."

"I hope so," Finn murmured.

He leaned forward and gently kissed her temple, then moved down, his lips barely touching the bruised skin of her face. When he reached her lips he carefully kissed her, so lightly his lips barely brushed against hers.

He moved to sit back but Lucy reached up to cup his head in her hand and brought him back to her. She kissed him again, lightly at first, and then more insistently. Finn tried to pull away again.

"Don't stop," Lucy begged.

"Lucy, we shouldn't."

"Why not? I've waited to be with you for nearly a decade. I'm done waiting."

She pulled him back to meet her lips, taking a long, deep taste of him.

"I don't want to hurt you," he murmured against her mouth.

She nipped at his bottom lip. "I'll tell you if it hurts."

He trailed kisses along her throat, down her neck. "Promise?"

He reached her collarbone, his tongue darting out to taste the hollow of her throat while he untied the ribbon of her neckline.

Lucy dragged in a tremulous breath. "I promise," she said, knowing she'd gladly suffer in silence before she'd tell him to stop what he was doing.

She leaned into him with a tremulous sigh, enjoying the warmth of his body pressed against hers. They were finally alone.

That notion pushed all thoughts from her mind. She gazed at him, her breath quickening as he leaned down to kiss her. The gentle press of his lips deepened, his tongue lightly flicking at her lips until she opened to him. His hands moved to cup her face, slipping into her hair and grabbing hold as he worshipped her with his lips.

Lucy's arms wound around Finn's neck, and she clung to him, her tongue tangling with his as a low moan escaped her throat. The small noise seemed to spur him on and her head swam as his hands massaged their way down her back, gripping her hips to keep them firmly pressed to him. She was very aware that he was every bit as affected as she. The heat building low in her belly flared as Finn covered her body with his own. She threw her head back, dragging in a ragged breath as he pushed her chemise off her shoulders, baring her to his touch. His hands traveled up her rib cage and she gasped, arching into his fingers as he gently caressed her through her thin gown.

Finn paused at the sound, glancing at her to make sure she was still okay. Lucy answered him by wrapping a leg about his hips and covering his lips with hers.

Neither one of them needed to have worried. Finn was extra-careful of her as he explored her body. Lucy felt nothing but sublime happiness. Any discomfort melted away on wave after wave of pleasure. She'd waited so very long for this moment, for this man. The love she felt for him eclipsed everything else. There was nothing but him, nothing but *them*. All the years of wondering, mourning, were burned away with every searing kiss, every whispered endearment.

And at the final moment, when Lucy gazed up at Finn to see her own tears of joy mirrored in his eyes, she knew they were both healed at last.

The day had waned into night and the morning dawned anew and still they lay tangled together. Lucy stretched out beside Finn and wrapped her arm around his waist, cuddling into him. He drew a finger along her jawline, pressing up on her chin to tilt her face up to his. He kissed her, his lips lingering long enough that the sweet hello began to build into something much more. Lucy brought her hand up to tangle in his hair, trying to press him even closer.

Finn chuckled and kissed the top of her head. "I should probably go. It'll be morning soon."

"Not yet," Lucy said, tightening her grip on him. "We've still got time."

Finn chuckled. "Possibly, though I'm not sure what we could do to fill that time. You've exhausted me, lass."

Lucy buried her smile against his chest, pressing a kiss to his collarbone. "We could talk."

"Hmm, about what?"

"You never told me how you got these," Lucy said, tracing the scars that ran over his chest and arms. "Or this." She ran a finger down a long scar on his leg and Finn shivered and laughed, snagging her hand so she couldn't do it again.

"Not much to tell. I fought in the war. Sometimes the war got the best of me."

"About that," Lucy said, propping herself up on her elbows. "If you work for Philip, who is Southern through and through, how in the world did you end up fighting for the North?"

Finn sighed and tucked a hand behind his head. "Philip thought if he had a man in a prominent position with the other army, it would give the South a leg up."

"You were a spy?"

Finn laughed again. "Not a very good one. I passed along enough information to keep Halford happy, but I made sure it was outdated. Headquarter locations that had been moved, plans that had been changed. A few times I even managed to feed them information that helped the North."

"Sounds like a fine line to balance."

"You have no idea," he said, leaning down to nuzzle at her neck.

"Hmm," she purred, the sensation of his breath on her neck toe-curlingly divine. "A butler, a double spy, a bodyguard, a priest. Is there anything you can't do?"

Finn snorted. "A priest?"

Lucy grinned. "You married Brynne and Jake, didn't you?"

"Well, yes. But I'm hardly a priest. Don't have the temperament for it," he said, swooping in for another kiss. "They were the only couple I ever married and it was really more of a mishmash of the few words I remembered from a handfasting I'd seen once in Ireland and the Mohave ceremonies I'd seen. And I only did it because Jake begged me to."

"I don't see why he even asked. He knew it wouldn't be legal."

Finn shrugged. "I suspect they just wanted something to make it more official in their eyes. A way to pledge themselves to each other until they could get a real pastor to do the job. I was the only somewhat religious man available at the time."

"A religious man, huh? Is that how you got these?" she asked, tracing the T-shaped tattoos just below Finn's cheekbones.

He took her hand and kissed her fingers, one by one, before laying her hand on his chest beneath his. The gesture was sweet, but Lucy knew he'd done it to stop her from touching the marks. She curled onto her side, her head propped on her arm.

"Is it a painful memory?"

"Yes."

Lucy's brow furrowed. She didn't understand. The marks were supposedly only given to very important members of the tribe. Gaining such marks, especially for one who was adopted into the tribe, should have been a wonderful memory. One to be proud of. Curiosity ate at her, but Lucy didn't want to pry further.

Finn sighed and wrapped his arm about her, drawing her into his chest. She loved being close to him, even though he'd effectively made it impossible for her to continue staring at him. The man had talent.

"Do you remember when you asked if I'd ever loved anyone before?"

Lucy held perfectly still, not sure where this was going, but not wanting to interrupt the first mention he'd made of his life before Boston.

"Yes," she answered quietly.

Finn's arms tightened around her and Lucy stroked his chest, trying to ease whatever turmoil was making his heart slam against her fingers.

"I called her Rachel. I couldn't pronounce her name when we first met." He smiled sadly. "She was the first one to smile at me when my mother and I first came to the village. The only one to smile at me. My mother and I...not everyone accepted our presence right away. Couldn't blame them, really. Two scraggly castoffs without another soul in the world to claim them. Except my stepfather, for a time at least.

"He'd found us half-starved outside one of the mining camps. My father had gotten sick on the crossing over from Ireland to America and the long journey to California hadn't improved his health. He died soon after we arrived in California. My mother was afraid to venture too far into the mining camp. Women were very scarce in those parts. She'd likely have had a hundred marriage proposals after her first afternoon, but she was convinced she'd be raped and left for dead if she set foot in the camp. She might have been right. So, whenever we needed supplies, I'd go in and barter or buy what I could, steal what I had to. We panned our little stream and kept to ourselves."

"How old were you?"

"Thirteen."

"So young," Lucy said, burrowing closer into Finn's chest. Her heart broke for the little boy he'd been.

"And how young were you when you started running raids with your sisters?"

Lucy laughed a little. "Okay, touché. So, how did you end up with the Mohave? They are much farther south than the mining camps."

"Yes. My stepfather was a trapper and a bit of a wanderer. He'd spend fall and winter trapping in the north and then would travel south, selling his furs and whatever else he'd scrounged up. He was a tinker of sorts, I suppose. Had a great cart full of all sorts of things. He came across my mother one afternoon when I was away. But he was kind to her, fed her, and me when I returned. He was a good man, took care of us. I liked him well enough. I think my mother was just relieved to have someone take over the job of provider. She was a kind, sweet woman but didn't have a tenth of your strength or gumption."

Lucy pressed a kiss against Finn's chest and let her fingers trail through the hair scattered across his skin. "He took you to the tribe?"

"Yes. We'd been planning to make our way back north, but my mother discovered she was pregnant. My stepfather thought it would be safer to stay put for a while. He often traded with the tribes and he brought us to one of the villages. They agreed to take us in until my mother's child was born."

Finn's voice had grown sad again and Lucy knew what he'd say before he uttered the words.

"My mother wasn't strong to begin with and all the traveling…well, it was just too much I guess. She died trying to give birth. The baby died with her."

"Oh, Finn. I'm so sorry."

His arms tightened for a moment, but he didn't stop, as though he wanted to get through the rest of the story as quickly as possible. "My stepfather stuck around for a few weeks, but he wasn't the type to stay in one place long. And without my mother there…well. He did make sure I would be accepted into the village before he left. One of the women in the tribe who'd lost a son adopted me. After a time, they gave me these," he said, pointing to the lines beneath his lip. "I was glad to have them. They made me feel like I belonged.

"I was happy there. I had friends. And Rachel. She and I were always together. She could speak English better than most of the others. She helped me learn Mohave. We were best friends. And then…we were more than that."

Finn stopped. The silence stretched long enough that Lucy didn't think he'd go on. But she didn't want to prompt him. Reliving his past was obviously painful for him and Lucy wasn't going to push. She wasn't so sure she wanted to hear the rest. So much pain in his young life. And yet, whatever happened to his first love, whatever memory was connected with the marks on his cheeks, was enough to make her stalwart warrior hesitate. Maybe she wasn't strong enough to hear it.

When he began to speak again, his voice was so low Lucy had to strain to hear it.

"I wasn't the only one in the village who loved her. There was another. One more worthy, in everyone's eyes but hers. The tribe's greatest warrior. But she loved me. Her family didn't approve. Who was I? I'd been made part of the tribe, yes. But I was different. I didn't really belong. So, we decided to run away.

"We snuck off one night. He followed us. Caught up with us. I fought him."

He stopped and cleared his throat, his grip on Lucy so tight it was almost painful, but she wouldn't have asked him to let go in a million years.

"I lost."

He was quiet again, but this time Lucy had to ask. Had to

know. "What happened?"

"Rachel tried to defend me, tried to help. A blow meant for me struck her. She fell on a rock. When he saw what he'd done, he went wild. I went numb. I don't remember much of what happened after that. I just kept seeing her, lying there in her own blood. I didn't fight him. I barely felt the blows. I wanted to die. Wanted to join her. But he wasn't that merciful. I was injured. Badly enough that I drifted in and out of consciousness for days. He was always there when I woke. I didn't understand why until I'd recovered enough to know what he'd done.

"He gave me these," Finn said, tracing his own finger over the marks this time. "He was returning to the village, to tell them what I'd done. Tell them that her death was on my head. I didn't even argue with him. He was right."

"Oh, Finn, it wasn't your fault."

"Yes, it was. I'd taken her away from the safety of the village. I'd thought I could protect her. That I would be enough. We didn't make it two days."

Lucy wanted to argue, insist that he was wrong. But she knew he wouldn't listen. Not yet. "What did you do?"

"I couldn't go back. I wouldn't have anyway, but with the marks on my cheeks, the marks that only the most important members of the tribe carried. No. I couldn't face them. It would be as if I'd been trying to set myself up above my place in the tribe. Mocking their sacred traditions. And I had Rachel's blood on my hands. At least they would believe so. No. I couldn't go back."

"How old were you?"

"Nineteen."

"Oh, Finn."

"I couldn't go back to them. But I couldn't go to any of the towns either. The marks made me an outcast among the townsfolk, though for an entirely different reason. I tried to find work where I could. But most took one look at my face and chased me off. Some took pity. I suppose if I had pretended that I'd been a captive that had escaped, things would have gone easier. I would have been pitied, not reviled. But I couldn't do that. They had been my family.

"So, I wandered. Did what I had to in order to survive. Begged and stole. Got into trouble. One day, got into too much trouble and ended up with a bounty on my head."

"And then you met Jake," Lucy said with a sad smile.

"Yes. Jake saved my life. I'll never know why he didn't turn me in. I remember him standing there, staring down at me. He asked if I knew why he was there. I said I sure did and held out my hands, waiting for him to tie me up and drag me in. But he didn't. He cleaned me up, fed me, clothed me. Got me back on my feet and helped me find work, vouched for me and put his own name on the line when folks balked at hiring me. He made me care about living again."

"Jake was a good man," Lucy said, smiling at the memory of Brynne's first husband.

"Yes, he was. And I failed him, too."

Lucy sat up so she could look into Finn's eyes. "No, Finn. You didn't fail him. What happened to Jake was not your fault. You weren't even in the country when he died. You couldn't have saved him. You'd probably have been killed along with him."

Finn stared sadly at her, brought his hand up to cup her face. "You're a good woman, Lucy. You deserve better than me. I bring only misery and destruction to anyone I care about. Now you see why you should leave, get away from me?"

Lucy was already shaking her head. "No. You're wrong, Finn. You are the best man I know. You are loyal, and brave, and strong. You have a kind heart and a warrior's spirit. I'm not a little girl who knows nothing of the world. I've seen the evil that is out there. And I've seen the good. You, my love, are the best of them all. Sweet heaven, to have gone through all you've been through and to still have your capacity for love and kindness is a testament to just how amazing a man you are. If it takes me the rest of my life, I'm going to convince you of that."

Finn started to shake his head, but Lucy grasped his face in her hands and forced him to look at her. "I'm a Richardson. We don't back down and we never give up. You aren't ever getting rid of me, Finnegan Taggart. Get used to it."

A small grin broke through the frozen lines of his face and Finn crushed Lucy to him, wrapping his whole body around her. Lucy untangled herself enough to reach his lips, trying to put every ounce of love she felt into her kiss. She breathed him in, let her hands explore the planes of his body, ingraining every inch into her memory. She tried to put into words all the love she felt for him and when that failed her, she showed him with her body how much he meant to her.

Finn pulled her beneath him, brushed her hair out of her face. "I don't deserve you."

Lucy just smiled. "You're right. You deserve someone far better than me."

"Well, we'll just have to agree to disagree on that one."

Lucy stretched beneath him and he bit his lip and bent to nuzzle her neck.

"Luckily, there are other things we can agree on."

"Hmm," Lucy purred. "Show me."

"Gladly."

He bent his head to kiss her.

Lucy heard Lilah's scream seconds before the door burst open.

"Well, now isn't this a cozy sight. Awfully inappropriate way to be treating your own cousin now, isn't it, Taggart?"

Philip stood in the doorway, a gun trained on them.

"Halford! What are you doing here?"

Finn jumped out of bed, shoving his legs into his pants. He threw Lucy's chemise at her, but when he reached for his shirt, and the gun that lay beneath it, Philip stopped him.

"I think you are decent enough," he said, gesturing with his gun for Finn to move away from his weapon.

His gaze flicked to Lucy, his eyes lingering on her bare shoulders. The leer on his face made her skin crawl and she grabbed her chemise and dragged it on as quickly as she could. That was the only movement Philip allowed her.

"What do you want, Halford?"

Philip looked back at Finn. "A few, shall we say discrepancies in the stories you've told me have been made known to me. First of all, you," he said, pointing the gun at Lucy, "aren't exactly who you say you are. In fact, far from being our Mr. Taggart's innocent cousin, you are not a Taggart at all, are you? Now, why you'd keep the fact that you are a Richardson from me is something I'd love to hear. But first I have a few matters I'd like to discuss with you," he said, aiming the gun at Finn.

"It seems several of my men have gone missing. And you haven't shown your face in my office since their disappearance. You can see why I assume you might have had something to do with it. When I couldn't find you at the hotel, I naturally assumed you might be keeping your delightful *cousin* company."

"You have no business being here. If you want me, fine. Wait outside and I'll be along momentarily."

"I'm afraid I can't do that. You see, it appears as though our dear Miss Taggart...excuse me, Miss Richardson, may have found herself in a bit of a compromising position the other night. I'm afraid I can't let such a breach of manners go."

Philip held up Lucy's earring, smiling coldly at her.

"An earring doesn't prove anything, Philip."

"Oh, I think it does." He cocked his head, scrutinizing her.

"How ever did you come by those dreadful injuries? You do look appalling, my dear."

Lucy surged up out of the bed, ignoring the pistol that was now aimed at her. "You know exactly what happened to me, Philip. And I'm fairly certain you know about the burned-out cross someone left at my school as well."

"I'm afraid I don't know what you are talking about."

"Yes, you do, you cowardly little worm of a man."

Philip hissed and raised his arm a fraction higher. "You might want to watch your tongue, my dear. You are wearing my patience very thin."

"Why should I? You don't have the guts to do your own dirty work. Not with your face exposed to the world at least. Missing any bed sheets, are you?"

Philip sneered at her, his fury palpable. "You miserable little bitch."

He raised the gun. Finn shouted and dove between them just as Philip fired. Finn jerked, crashing to the floor with a stream of blood running from his head.

Lucy screamed and crouched beside Finn, using her chemise to stanch the flow of blood.

"Don't worry. You're next."

Philip raised his arm again. There was a loud cracking sound and Philip's eyes widened. His mouth went slack and his eyes glazed over. The gun fell from his hand as he toppled forward onto the floor.

Lilah stood behind him, a heavy iron frying pan dangling from her hand.

"Lilah," Lucy whispered.

"Is he dead?" she asked.

Lucy looked at Philip. The back of his head had been smashed nearly flat. His chest was motionless. But Lilah's gaze wasn't on Philip. It was on Finn.

"No," Lucy said, feeling the steady rise and fall of his

chest beneath her fingers. "No, he's not dead."

"Good." Lilah stood still in the doorway, her face blank. Lucy didn't know if she was horrified or just stunned by what she'd just done. But they were going to have company very shortly and the maid couldn't be found standing over Philip's body with the murder weapon.

"Lilah, you need to go. Quickly. Whoever Philip brought with him will have heard the gunshot. They'll be coming soon when he doesn't reappear."

She spoke more urgently, trying to break through the haze Lilah seemed to be in. "Lilah! Listen to me. You need to go. Take the frying pan and throw it away or hide it. But don't be seen with it. Go. Now!"

Finally her words broke through. Lilah shook her head. "I can't be leavin' you. They'll think you did this. You can't take the blame."

"I'll be fine," Lucy promised, though she didn't know if she believed that or not. "I can explain. I'll tell them it was self-defense. Finn has been shot and Philip was the one with the gun. That will prove it was self-defense. But if they see you, standing there like that…they won't listen."

Lilah nodded. She knew Lucy was right. "You'll be all right?"

"I'll be fine. Now go, quickly!"

Lilah turned and ran out of the bedroom. The back door off the kitchen slammed shut and Lucy prayed she'd get away before Philip's men came.

It didn't take long. Two men came in and Lucy's heart dropped. There would be no bribing or bullying them into forgetting what they were seeing.

They took one look at Philip and Finn, in all his tattooed glory, lying half naked on the floor, and Lucy standing between them covered in blood.

And all hell broke loose.

Chapter Fifteen

The looks on the men's faces would have been comical if it all wasn't so tragic. They both pulled guns from beneath their coats and began shouting and searching for someone to point the weapons at. But there was no one but Finn, who was unconscious on the floor, and Lucy, a woman they obviously didn't consider a threat. They finally seemed to work out that if Finn was incapacitated, then Lucy must have done the murderous deed.

One of them, an older portly gentleman with a waistcoat stretched so tightly across his midsection that Lucy feared the buttons would pop off, tried to wave her away from Finn, but she refused to budge. He seemed at a loss of what to do. He glanced at his partner.

"Make her move. We need to tie her up until the sheriff gets here."

"I don't know, Jed. She looks like she's been worked over a bit, too. Maybe it wasn't her."

Lucy started at the name, her gaze shooting to the other man, who was younger, not quite as thick, though his waistcoat showed signs of strain as well.

"Jed?"

The younger man looked at her with a sneer.

"Have we met?" she asked, her voice dripping with ice and fury.

He smiled at her, like a cobra would smile at a fuzzy, white rabbit, and Lucy's belly dropped. The older gentleman might hesitate to harm her, but this one…he wasn't so conflicted and wanted her to know it. He didn't answer her but turned back to his companion.

"Come on, Thomas. Who else could it be? The savage there couldn't have done it. I doubt poor Halford could get off a shot after he got hit like that. Must have happened before, and there isn't anyone else here who could have done it. Isn't that right, missy?"

Lucy hesitated. She didn't want to implicate Lilah. But she didn't want to go to jail for a murder she didn't commit either. She hadn't really thought that far into her plan when she'd told Lilah to run though she knew that she had a better chance than Lilah of getting a fair hearing. She'd just have to tell as much of the truth as she could and hope that someone would believe her. She had no illusions about the two in front of her. Or at least about Jed. He looked like he'd gladly hang her right there and then.

"No, that isn't right. I didn't hurt Philip. He burst in and shot Finn and was going to attack me as well. Someone hit him over the head before he could and then ran. I…didn't see who it was. I was too busy trying to help Finn."

"Well now, that's convenient, isn't it?"

"Wait a minute. Did you say Finn? Is that Finn Taggart down there?" Thomas took a step forward, his gaping mouth creating a third chin as he stared down at Finn. "Well, I'll be."

"It doesn't matter who is down there, Thomas. She killed him."

"That's Taggart, Jed. Something's not adding up here. Taggart's Halford's right-hand man. Why would Halford shoot him?"

Jed looked at Lucy, his eyes roving over her from head to toe. "Oh, I reckon I could think of a few reasons."

Thomas followed his gaze, frowning. "You think they'd try and kill each over a woman?"

"No, I don't. I think Taggart was poaching Halford's territory. Halford has been escorting her all over town. And you know the temper on him. So what do you think he'd do if he came in and saw that his best man had beat him to the prize, eh? She looks like she took a lick or two as well. I wouldn't put it past Halford to teach the little trollop a lesson if she was stepping out on him. She always did seem a might too full of herself. Instead of taking what was coming to her like a good little girl, maybe she waited until Halford's back was turned and then she done him in."

Thomas looked dubious, but the first threads of worry for herself were edging through her fear for Finn. Jed's story actually seemed fairly plausible. And it wasn't far from the truth. Only Halford hadn't done the beating and Lucy hadn't done the killing. But Lucy didn't know how many people would stop to listen to that. Jed's theory explained everything and with Lucy and Finn already in custody, as she was sure they would both be shortly, it saved the authorities a lot of trouble.

Jed smiled at her, obviously coming to the same conclusion. "I think you'd better come with us, Miss Taggart."

Lucy hesitated. She didn't want to leave Finn lying there. And she had no intention of going anywhere in only a bloodstained chemise.

"I'm not going anywhere with the two of you."

"Oh, yes you are," Jed said, taking a menacing step toward her.

"You have no authority to make me go anywhere. I told you the truth. I didn't kill Philip and obviously neither did Finn. If you don't believe me, fine. Go and get the sheriff. But I'm not going anywhere with *you*."

Jed ground his teeth and for a second Lucy thought he might force her to leave with him. But Thomas spoke up before Jed could do something stupid.

"She's right, Jed. We can't just haul her down to the jailhouse. Besides, the sheriff will want to have a look at all this."

"Fine then," Jed ground out. "Go and fetch him."

Lucy's sudden panic at being left alone must have shown on her face because Thomas hesitated.

"Perhaps it would be best if we sent someone else. That way we are both here as witnesses. So we can be sure nothing is tampered with."

Thomas had a hard edge to his voice that wasn't there before. Maybe he'd finally picked up on Jed's hostility toward Lucy. Whether he thought she was a murderess or not, he was at least willing to spare her Jed's particular brand of justice.

"Well then, send one of the Negroes that's hanging around out in the front. There are enough of them to choose from. And send one of the women in here to help get this mess cleaned up."

"I don't think we should clean anything up until—"

"Fine, whatever! But we can't just leave him lying there like that. He needs to be covered up or something."

Thomas glanced between Jed and Lucy and then hurried out the door. Lucy tightened her hold on Finn, protecting him from anything Jed might do as much as needing the comfort.

Finn stirred and Lucy risked taking her eyes off Jed for a quick peek. Finn didn't wake, but there was some color returning to his face. Lucy took that as a good sign.

Thomas was back in moments, towing a woman behind

him. Lucy looked up and met Ruby's gaze. Ruby glanced quickly about the room, took in Lucy in her blood-splattered clothing, Finn unconscious in her lap, and Philip dead on the floor, and nodded her head.

She grabbed a sheet off the bed and managed to shoo Jed and Thomas out the door so she could cover Philip with it. They stayed in the cottage, but they were out of Lucy's eyesight and for that she was grateful.

Ruby grabbed a skirt and blouse and brought them over to Lucy. "I reckon you'll be asked to go along with the lawmen once they get here, miss. Best be presentable."

Lucy looked down at Finn.

"Don't you worry about him. He's a strong one. He be just fine. And he be the first to want you covered if you have to go with those men."

Well, now that was the truth at least. Lucy eased Finn onto the floor, taking a last look at the wound on his head. The bleeding had nearly stopped and though Finn was pale, his breathing was slow and steady.

She stood and let Ruby help her get dressed. She would have liked to don a clean chemise, but she didn't know how much time she had and would rather have a dress on top than a clean chemise underneath.

"Did you see Lilah?" Lucy asked.

"Don't you worry none about her, neither. She got away safe. Thanks to you."

"Good." Lucy sighed. At least one person in this whole debacle would be out of harm's way.

"You sure it was a good idea to send her away?"

Lucy nodded. "You know what would have happened to her if she'd stayed. They'll at least listen to me. They might not believe me," Lucy said with a tremulous smile, "but they'll listen. They wouldn't have given Lilah that courtesy. I doubt they'd have even taken her in for a trial."

Ruby nodded, her eyes filling with tears. "You're a good woman, Miz Lucy. You need anything, you just let me know."

The sound of hoofbeats echoed from the courtyard and Lucy glanced down at Finn. "Take care of him for me."

Then she walked out the door to face whatever consequences awaited her.

. . .

Finn woke slowly, the dull throbbing in his skull worsening the more aware he became. He risked cracking an eye open, blinking to clear his vision. He was still in Lucy's house, in her bed.

Lucy!

He sat up, holding a hand to his head to keep it from exploding, and flipped the blankets back.

Ruby ran in, took one look at him, and attempted to shove him back under the covers. "Don't you even think of it, Mr. Taggart. You get yourself right back in there."

"Lucy…"

"Don't you be worrin' about her just now. You need to get yourself healed up or Miz Lucy'll never forgive me."

Finn gently pushed her away and stood up, leaning a hand against the headboard until his head stopped spinning. It still throbbed, but it was manageable. "Where is she?"

Ruby pursed her lips. "Lord, but you're a stubborn man."

"Ruby…"

She held her hands up in defeat. "All right, all right. But here, drink this." She shoved a glass of water from the bedside table at him. Finn accepted it and drank, grateful for the coolness that washed away the feeling of cotton in his mouth. The water helped the ache in his head a bit too. Now…

Ruby frowned. "She's down at the jailhouse."

"She's what?" Finn shouted, flinching at the renewed pain

in his temples.

"She been arrested for murderin' Mr. Halford."

Finn sank to the bed, too stunned to react.

Ruby took a cautious step forward. "You all right, Mr. Finn?"

"Halford's dead?"

Ruby nodded, her worry still creasing her forehead.

"Lucy killed him?"

"No..." Ruby said hesitantly.

"Lilah?" Ruby didn't answer, but Finn already knew the answer. If Lucy hadn't done it, there was no one else who could have. Or would have.

"Why was Lucy arrested?"

"His men found her in here, covered in blood."

"Blood? Was she hurt?"

"No, sir. It was your blood."

"Oh," Finn said, putting his hand to his head. The pain creasing through it had faded in the wake of Ruby's revelation. It was still present, but compared to the pain lancing through his heart, it didn't matter.

It was happening again. The woman he loved had been left to face her mortal enemy while he'd be out cold on the ground. Arrested for the murder of a prominent politician? She'd been found with the body, with no witnesses to prove anyone else had done the deed. They'd hang her for sure.

Bile rose in Finn's throat and he stumbled out of the bedroom into the kitchen. He went straight for the whiskey he'd seen on Lucy's shelf. She wasn't a drinker. She probably used it for medicinal purposes only. But he needed it now.

He wrenched off the cap and took a slug that made his eyes water. The smooth fire running down his throat burned off some of the panic that was clouding his mind and he took another drink.

Ruby stood watching him, her arms crossed over her

chest. "That won't help anyone, especially Miz Lucy. You try to see her with you all covered in blood and stumblin' drunk and they'll lock you up right along with her. What good will that do anybody?"

"I have no intention of getting drunk," Finn said, taking one last pull on the bottle before replacing it on the shelf. He could hold his liquor. His stepfather had let him take shots of his whiskey before he was old enough to shave. But it did steady him, calmed the nerves that were wrangling out of control.

He couldn't lose her. *He couldn't.*

Finn took a deep breath, shoving his roiling emotions back in the deep corner of his heart, and started for the door.

"Where you goin'?" Ruby asked.

"To get Lucy the hell out of that jail."

"You can't go lookin' like that!"

Finn looked down and realized that he was still wearing his bloodstained pants.

"I patched up your head but you didn't have new clothes here. Sam's gone to the hotel to fetch your things. He'll be back soon."

Finn closed his eyes, breathing deeply through the urge to bolt from the house. His panic over Lucy hovered just under the surface and it took every ounce of strength he had to keep it from overwhelming him.

Luckily, Sam entered carrying a small case of clothing. Finn nodded his thanks and grabbed the case. Sam talked to him through the door of the bedroom as he changed his soiled clothing.

"I checked in at the jailhouse. Figured you'd want word of Miz Lucy."

Bless the man. "How is she?"

"They wouldn't let me in. Said visitin' weren't allowed 'til three. But I got a cousin that works for the sheriff, cleaning up the cells and such. He tole me Miz Lucy doin' as fine as can be expected. She look scared, but she holdin' up real well."

Finn stopped, his hands twitching with the fury and fear that flooded him. His Lucy was sitting in a cell, scared and alone. And he'd be damned if he'd let them keep him away from her.

Once he'd gotten dressed and looked somewhat respectable, he threw the door open and stalked out.

"Thanks, Sam."

Sam nodded, following behind him as Finn stormed outside and went to his horse.

"You can't go visitin' for another hour, Mr. Finn."

"I don't care when visiting hours are, Sam."

Finn swung up into his saddle ignoring the worried looks Sam and Ruby exchanged.

"Now, Mr. Finn, I know you want to go bustin' in there, but it just won't do nobody any good," Ruby said. "But Miz Lucy goin' to be needin' more help than you can give her. She needs one of them fancy lawyers, and I'm sure she'd feel better if her family could be here with her. Somebody needs to be seein' to those things."

Finn nearly screamed his frustration out loud. Ruby was right. He knew she was. But the only thing he wanted was to ride straight to that jail and get Lucy out of there.

"I'll go with you to the telegraph station, sir. And then we can go to the jail. If they still won't let you in, maybe my cousin can arrange somethin," Sam offered.

Finn sat for a moment, his horse pawing at the ground in imitation of Finn's agitation.

Finally, Finn nodded. As much as he'd like to tear that jailhouse down brick by brick, that just wasn't going to happen. Lucy's best chance was for her highfalutin lawyer to come and get her out of this mess. And she would feel much better with her sisters here.

Sam released a sigh of relief and ran to mount his horse. Finn pulled his horse around and thundered off toward town, Sam close on his heels.

. . .

Lucy paced the jail cell, worry over Finn eating at her until she felt she'd go mad from it. She hadn't heard from anyone, hadn't even seen anyone since the sheriff had locked her in the cell. They were treating her as if...well, as if she'd just bashed in a man's head with a frying pan.

She slumped onto the narrow cot shoved against the wall. They hadn't even let her wash the blood from her hands. She'd wiped them down as best she could before they'd taken her off, but there was still blood caked beneath her fingernails and a few odd spots here and there. She rubbed at her hands, watching the tiny flakes of Finn's blood flutter to the floor.

Where was he? *How* was he? The bullet had only grazed him, but it had bled so horribly. Had he woken yet? She had no idea what had happened to him.

Everything after the sheriff and his men had arrived was a bit of a blur. They'd marched in, and any sympathy they'd had for Lucy disappeared once they had seen Philip's body. Unfortunately, they seemed to be subscribing to Jed's interpretation of the scene and nothing that Lucy said prevailed. No matter that Philip was the one who was trespassing on her property, with a loaded weapon that he'd used to shoot Finn. Since Lucy had been openly courting Philip, the consensus seemed to be that Philip had every right to lose his mind in a fit of jealousy over finding Lucy with Finn.

Lucy's true identity had been revealed as well, a fact that made anyone inclined to give her the benefit of the doubt change their minds. Here she'd been in their midst all this time, masquerading as Finn's cousin when in fact she was Miss Lucy Richardson, a lying Yankee who couldn't be trusted. Coupled with the fact that she'd been found with a naked Finn in her bedroom and Lucy's stature was vastly reduced in their eyes. She was no longer an innocent young woman who needed to be coddled and protected. She was a wanton, deceitful woman who'd seduced not one but two men, and had driven them to this bloody battle. And since there was no one else coming forward to confess to the murder, Lucy had been formally arrested and charged with the murder of Philip Halford.

She couldn't blame them really. But that didn't stop the fear from gnawing at her.

The outer door opened and Lucy went to the barred door of her cell, straining to see who had come.

When she saw Finn walk around the corner, she nearly collapsed in relief.

"You're all right," she said, sticking her hand through the bars to grasp his.

Finn raised her hand to his lips and put his hand through the bars to caress her cheek.

"How are you?" he asked.

"I'm fine. I've been worried about you. But other than that, I'm fine."

"They haven't been mistreating you?"

"No. In fact, I haven't seen anyone at all since they locked me in here. What is happening? They aren't arresting you, are they?"

Finn shook his head. "They'd like to, but try as they might, they couldn't come up with a plausible story to explain how I could have been shot *after* hitting Halford. The only logical explanation is that he shot first and then someone else attacked him…which proves my innocence."

His worried eyes met Lucy's and Lucy tightened her grip

on his hand. "But my innocence isn't so easy to prove, hmm?"

Finn's face hardened. "We *will* prove it. You didn't do anything. I'm not going to let you be charged for someone else's crime."

Lucy smiled at him, hoped it reached her eyes. She appreciated his sentiment, but they both knew that proving her innocence would be difficult. If not impossible. If she hadn't been in that room, even she wouldn't believe in her innocence. For a split second, she wished she hadn't sent Lilah away. She was instantly overcome with shame. Lilah would probably not even have had the benefit of a trial. Judging by the number of men who had come to visit her school what seemed like a lifetime ago, Lucy was only too sure there were plenty of folks who would have meted out their vigilante justice before cooler heads could prevail.

At least Lucy had a fighting chance. She hoped.

"It might be time to contact my sisters," Lucy said.

Finn ran his thumb over her bruised cheek. "I already wired them. They wouldn't let me come in until three," he said, his voice thick with anger. "So I used the time to send a few telegrams. I also contacted a friend of mine, Mr. William Fitzhugh. He's one of the best lawyers in these parts. He should be here shortly."

"Thank you, Finn."

Finn shook his head and looked down, swallowing audibly a few times. "I'm so sorry, Lucy."

Lucy's eyes widened and she gripped his hand tighter, reaching through the bars to cup his face and bring his gaze back to hers. "For what?"

"This is my fault."

"How on earth do you figure that?"

"I should have stayed away from you. I knew I'd only bring you trouble. If I hadn't been there…"

"In case you haven't noticed, I seem to be fairly adept at

getting myself into trouble." She pointed to her battered face with a wry smile, but Finn flinched.

"Finn, it was only a matter of time before Philip confronted me, or I him. The only reason I allowed him to court me was so I could pry into his affairs and I'm fairly certain he knew that. This," she said, indicating her face, "happened because I was too careless when I was butting my nose into his business. And what happened at my house…that was no one's fault but Philip's. *He* was the trespasser. *He* was the aggressor. *He* attacked *you*. We did nothing wrong. And I wouldn't give back a second of my time with you for anything in the world."

Finn leaned his forehead against the bars and Lucy did the same, hating the feel of the cold metal pressed against her skin. But she could feel some of Finn's warmth as well. It would have to be enough. For now.

"I must go for a bit. Mr. Fitzhugh is coming in on the six o'clock train and I'm sure your sisters will be on their way as well. I need to see if they've left any messages."

He tilted Lucy's head up, his fingers gently stroking from her jaw down her neck. "I can't stand to leave you in here."

Lucy forced a smile. "Go. I'll be fine."

Finn leaned his head against the bars and pressed his lips to hers. "I'll be back as quickly as I can."

She nodded and watched him walk away.

Lucy managed to keep her tears at bay until he'd disappeared from sight. She was going to have to be strong if she was going to get through this, strong enough to fight against those who would bring her down. Strong enough to convince Finn and her sisters, who she'd never been able to lie to, that she was confident and optimistic. Strong enough to convince herself.

But for now, for this moment, she'd let the weakness out. Get it out of her system so she could move past it. Because if she didn't get rid of it, it would bury her under the waves of despair and fear that threatened to consume her.

Standing on tiptoe so she could see outside, she watched as Finn came into view. He climbed into a waiting carriage and rode away.

When she could no longer see the carriage in the distance, Lucy sank to the floor and sobbed.

Chapter Sixteen

Finn paced the platform, waiting for the train that would bring Lucy's family. They'd been fortunate that Cilla and Leo had already been on the East Coast, visiting Leo's family in Maryland. Brynne and Richard had met up with them there and the foursome would be pulling into the station any minute.

When Finn heard the telltale whistle of the train as it approached the station, he stopped pacing, standing rigid as the train came into view. His stomach churned. He'd barely eaten or slept since Lucy had been in jail. Lucy was *his* responsibility. He was the reason she was in trouble, and he was going to make damn sure that Lucy went free, no matter the cost or the stakes. If her sisters could aid him in that, all the better. He wasn't too proud to accept help from her formidable family. But no matter what, he'd see Lucy safe.

Then again, the last time he'd seen Brynne, he'd been trying to collect a ransom for kidnapping her daughter. They hadn't exactly parted on the best of terms. No matter what Lucy said, Finn was still fairly certain Brynne would stake him through the heart as soon as look at him. But he needed help and Lucy needed her family. So, he'd just have to make sure Brynne's anger stayed focused on getting Lucy out of danger. Then she could have at him.

The train pulled to a stop and Finn squared his shoulders, mentally preparing for their arrival. He didn't have to wait long.

Cilla descended first, followed by her husband Leo. They'd never met, but Finn would know him anywhere. He looked very much like his brother Jake.

Finn went to them and stuck out his hand. "Mr. Forrester?"

Leo nodded and shook his hand. "You must be Mr. Taggart."

"Yes, sir."

Finn glanced at Cilla who was watching him thoughtfully, sizing him up. A natural thing to do, he supposed, seeing as how they were aware of his past with Lucy and her feelings for him. Though he couldn't help but feel she was taking his measure, not as a mate for her sister, but as an opponent on the battlefield.

Another man joined their group. He was tall and blond, with a pair of smart spectacles perched on his nose. Finn had forgotten he had someone else to be wary of. Richard Oliver was now Coraline's stepfather and had just as much reason as Brynne to despise Finn. But Richard approached him calmly, only a slight narrowing of his eyes indicating he wasn't entirely pleased to see Finn again.

Finn offered his hand. "Dr. Oliver."

Richard nodded and shook Finn's hand, though his expression was decidedly cool.

Richard turned to help his wife from the train, and Finn could no longer avoid the moment he'd been dreading.

Brynne stood before him, her gaze skewering him where he stood.

"Mrs. Oliver," he said, bowing his head a little, waiting for whatever she had to say. It had been a long time coming and he deserved every word.

Brynne eyed him up and down. "You look different without the tattoos showing."

Finn nodded, wary of her and a bit thrown off guard by the fact that she hadn't immediately attacked him. It had been several years, and Lucy *had* said that Brynne had forgiven him. Still…

"I like you better with them," she added.

Finn's lips twitched. "So do I. They do tend to make a man stand out though, and that's not something I want to do down here."

Brynne nodded. Her eyes zeroed in on the bruised and barely healed bullet wound on his head. "She try to shoot you?"

Finn couldn't help the smile that broke out. "No, ma'am. Someone tried to shoot her."

Brynne snorted. "Sounds about right. You put your own head in the way to protect her?"

Finn nodded.

"Is this mess she's in your doing?"

Finn wasn't sure how to answer that one. He hesitated and Brynne cocked an eyebrow.

"Yes and no."

The eyebrow raised higher. "Care to explain?"

"Brynne, leave the poor man alone," Cilla said. "You and I both know Lucy is more than capable of getting herself into a scrape like this. It's not like she's the only one of us to be arrested for a murder she didn't commit. We just have a knack for life-threatening tomfoolery. Can't blame Mr. Taggart here for that."

Brynne muttered something about her sisters being the death of her.

Finn's lips twitched. The Richardson sisters were quite a trio. "I wasn't directly responsible. But the man who attacked us was my boss and Lucy had…gotten on his bad side. She'd never have crossed his path if she hadn't been trying to get me to admit that I love her, so in a roundabout way, yes, this is my fault."

"And do you? Love her?" Brynne asked.

Finn frowned, his mouth hanging open. Her question was so unexpected, he wasn't sure at first he'd heard her correctly. "Pardon?"

"Do you love her?" she asked again, her fists on her hips.

Finn hadn't admitted it out loud yet and knew if he was going to say it to anyone, it should be to Lucy. But after everything he'd put her family through, no matter his reasons for doing it, he'd do anything for them. Answering a question that would put Brynne's mind at ease was the least he could do.

"Yes, ma'am. I do. Very much."

Brynne nodded again, apparently happy with his answers. "Well, then Mr. Taggart. I'd appreciate it if you could take us to the jailhouse."

Richard stepped forward. "Brynne, we should stop by the hotel first. It's been a long journey. You should rest a bit before we go over."

Brynne just looked at her husband. Cilla and Leo had turned their faces to hide their smiles and even Finn knew the poor man was going to lose this argument before it even began.

Richard drew his wife into his arms with an amused sigh and kissed her forehead. "You can't blame a man for trying."

"I most certainly could," she said, though her fond tone took the sting from her words.

"This way," Finn said, leading the way to the carriage he had waiting. He gave instructions for the boy he'd brought with him to have the Richardsons' and Forresters' luggage brought to the hotel where he'd already reserved a suite of rooms for them, and then held the door to the carriage open so they could climb inside.

They passed the short ride to the jailhouse in relative silence, each lost in their own thoughts. The momentary brevity at the station dissipated the closer to the jail they came. When they alighted in the jail's courtyard, the full gravity of the situation had overcome them once again.

Finn led the way. There was a short delay at the front desk because the officer in charge didn't want to allow the visitors access to Lucy unless they'd been thoroughly searched. Brynne stood there and stared the man down until he turned beet red and let them through with a cursory pat for the men and a polite nod for the women. Then, finally, they were led back to Lucy's cell.

...

Lucy heard the outer door open and sat up on her bunk, leaning forward to see who it was. Her lawyer had already been by earlier that morning. Their case was made more difficult since there were no witnesses, as Lucy refused to tell him Lilah's identity, to testify to Lucy's innocence, but Mr. Fitzhugh was still measurably hopeful they'd be able to exonerate her. Lucy wasn't quite so sure, but she was willing to go along with him for now. What else could she do?

When she saw her sisters walk through the door, she jumped from her bunk with a glad cry. Cilla and Brynne rushed to the door, waiting impatiently for the officer to open it, then fairly shoved the man aside so they could get to Lucy.

Lucy was smothered in two sets of arms. The men wisely stayed back. The sisters were all crying and talking at once, hugs and kisses and exclamations of love and exasperation at

Lucy's predicament flying about the room until Lucy finally had to wave her sisters back so she could get a word in edge wise.

"I can't believe you're here," she said, giving them both a firm hug and a kiss on the cheek. "You can't even imagine how happy I am to see you."

"Yes, we can," Cilla said with a smile. "Now, would you care to fill us in on exactly how our baby sister came down to North Carolina to find an old friend and ended up in jail for murder?"

Lucy took a deep breath and launched into the tale, leaving out nothing. When she'd finished, Brynne and Cilla glanced at each other, and then back to her.

"Mr. Taggart has informed us that you've retained a lawyer," Brynne said. "What does he say about all this?"

Lucy shrugged. "He's optimistic. I have no criminal past…" Cilla's eyebrows raised, the scar bisecting her left brow exaggerating her surprised look, and Lucy rolled her eyes and continued, "that anyone knows about. While here, I've been a good member of the community. The fact that I started the school could both help and hurt us, he thinks, depending on who's on the jury. On one hand, it shows my 'charitable' nature. But on the other hand…"

"On the other hand," Cilla filled in, "if you get a bunch of bigoted old-timers, the fact that you started a school to teach Negroes will go against you."

"Right."

"No one is questioning that Philip was the one who shot Finn, so Finn at least is safe from suspicion since it's a bit impossible for him to have bashed Philip in the head from behind *after* being shot. Believe me, I wasn't sure there for a while. When we were found, Finn didn't have his tattoos covered, which gave everyone a bit of a shock. I'm sure if they could have pinned some blame on him, they would have.

But there simply isn't any way to make an accusation stick, so that's a good bit of news."

"Sure. Good for Finn. But it doesn't help you," Richard said.

Lucy shot him a dirty look.

"Now don't go getting angry at Richard for just saying what we're all thinking. It's fine and dandy for Taggart to be above suspicion, but that still leaves you as the only suspect," Brynne said.

"Why can't you just tell them who really killed the man?" Leo asked. "Surely you must know."

"Of course I know. But I can't reveal who it is. She was only trying to protect me and I'm not going to let her hang for that."

"Lucy," Brynne said, drawing Lucy down to sit beside her and Cilla on the bench. "I know you want to protect this woman, but I think it's time for you to face the facts. You could be the one on the end of the rope. Are you prepared to just give up and die to keep her identity a secret?"

Lucy looked at Finn, a lump forming in her throat. "Of course I don't want to die. I don't want to spend the rest of my life, or even one more moment behind these bars. And I have no intention of just giving up. But there has to be some way of proving my innocence without giving her up in the process."

"Lucy," Finn said, kneeling down in front of her, "I spoke with Fitzhugh after he left you this morning. It doesn't look good. There was no one else there. If you don't tell them who really killed Halford, then in their minds, there is no one else who could have done it but you. Don't you see that? If you don't tell them who really killed him, you'll be the one hanging."

"Finn, I can't…"

"We have the best lawyer in the South on our side. And what happened to Halford was self-defense. Hell, no one is even questioning that the man shot me. That proves it was self-defense! There is no guarantee that she'll hang for this."

"And there's no guarantee that I will either. So why can't we just argue that defense for me? I've got a much better chance with a jury than she will."

"Because you have other motives for wanting him dead."

Lucy's blood ran cold. She'd never considered that the prosecution might have an actual case against her. She hadn't confessed and other than finding her with the body, covered in blood, and she knew how damning that looked, she didn't think they had anything on her.

"What possible motives could I have for wanting Philip dead? As far as the community was concerned, we were courting."

"Exactly. You were courting him and then were found in bed with me."

Brynne sucked in an angry breath and Lucy sighed. "Don't lecture me about that now, Brynne. You can give me the moral-deprivation sermon later."

Brynne's eyes narrowed, though her glare was directed at Finn, but she waved them on.

"So," Lucy continued, "because I was found with you, they think that is motive for murder?"

Finn grimaced and pulled a newspaper clipping out of his pocket. "I didn't want to show you these…"

He handed them to her and Lucy quickly read the article. The headline, **Schoolmistress Kills City Icon to Hide Illicit Affair** had her ready to chew glass before getting two sentences into the article. The so-called article was a sordid description painting her as a wanton hussy who'd set out to seduce the goodly Mr. Halford. He'd caught her in the arms of a savage, in the midst of some devilishly heathen lovemaking, they were sure to point out. Lucy, in a rage at Mr. Halford's rightful rejection of her upon discovering her betrayal, had killed him.

Lucy stared at the offensive trash in her hands. "Surely no one believes this filth?"

"Enough do. And it'll only take twelve to convict you."

"Lucy," Cilla said, taking her sister's hands. "You've got to tell them who really did this. I promise you we will do everything in our power to keep her safe. But your life is our priority here. And I think you need to seriously consider the possibility that you will be found guilty."

Lucy looked at Brynne and then at Richard and Leo. And finally at Finn.

"Only if you promise me that she won't hang. Even if we have to bust her out of here and go on the run. Promise me."

Finn took her face in his hands. "I swear to you, I will not let her hang for this."

Lucy stared into his eyes for a long moment. Nausea from guilt and fear rose in her gut, and she swallowed several times, trying to calm the furious pounding of her heart.

They were right though. She'd be found guilty. She would die.

Finally she nodded. "All right."

Finn crushed her to him. "It will be all right, love. For both of you." He set her from him so he could look into her eyes again. "I swear it."

"I hope you're right."

Chapter Seventeen

Finn flipped through the telegrams in his hand, though reading them again wouldn't change the messages they contained. He balled them up and threw them to the floor, not caring about the startled look the telegraph operator gave him.

Nothing. Richard and Leo and the team of men they'd hired to help search for Lilah had once again come up empty. They hadn't found one single solitary sign of Lilah. She had just vanished into thin air. No one had seen her and none of her friends and family would admit to knowing anything.

The rotten part of it was that Finn believed them. They seemed just as worried about Lilah and just as distressed over Lucy as Finn and Lucy's sisters. While they might not be too keen on Lilah turning herself in, they did very much want to help Lucy.

Finn raked his hand through his hair, trying to calm the growing panic in his gut. The case against Lucy was circumstantial, but it was a good one. Hell, if he was on the jury and heard the prosecution's salacious tale, he'd be riveted to his seat…and then he'd probably convict Lucy of murder.

She'd pled not guilty, of course, and her lawyer was making no secret of the fact that they were claiming that a third party had killed Halford in self-defense. But without any proof... well, it wasn't looking good.

Finn took a deep breath, shoved his emotions back into the dark pit they'd escaped from, and set off to deliver his bad news.

Brynne and Cilla took it about as he suspected. Brynne stared wide-eyed into the fire, seemingly in shock, though Finn knew her mind was thinking up and rejecting a hundred different options behind that blank stare.

Cilla was wearing a hole in the rug with her pacing. Finally, she stopped and threw up her hands.

"This is ridiculous! We can't just let them convict Lucy of murder."

Brynne blinked, completely unsurprised by her sister's outburst. "And just what do you suggest we do about it? March into the jail and demand her immediate release? Or perhaps we should organize an escape plan and spirit her away in the middle of the night."

"Yes! If that's our only option, then hell yes. Let's bust in there and get her."

Brynne sighed and sank back into the couch. "And what happens after that? Assuming we could get her out of there in the first place, and manage to get her out of the city without being caught, what then? Where will she go?"

"The same place you were going to send me when I was locked up for murders I didn't commit. She can go down to Mexico. Carmen and Miguel still have family there. They'd welcome her."

"When you were arrested, it was in California. Mexico wasn't that far away. Carmen's family is on the west coast of Mexico and we are on the east coast of the United States. It would take weeks to reach them, months maybe. And in the meantime, everyone and their blind Aunt Molly will be looking for her."

"So let them look! We'll hide her. If Mexico is too far away, send her up to Canada. Or we could smuggle her onto a boat and ship her to the Continent. You, Finn, you're from Ireland, you could take her there."

"I haven't been to Ireland since I was a child. Besides, getting her onto a boat and keeping her undetected throughout the voyage would be difficult," Finn said, hating to speak against her idea. He was all for spiriting Lucy away. But he wasn't sure where they could go where she'd be safe, if they could get her away at all.

"Difficult, but not impossible," Cilla insisted.

"Cilla," Brynne said, "this case is already the most notorious case the state has seen in a very long time. Her portrait has been splashed all over the papers with all those horrible articles. Lucy would have to look over her shoulder for the rest of her life, always worried that someone might recognize her and turn her in."

"Well at least she'd be alive enough to worry!" Cilla stood glaring at her sister, her breath coming in short pants. "I can't believe you're just willing to sit there and give up. You blew up half a town to save me from the end of a rope but you're not even willing to discuss doing the same for Lucy."

"Oh, Cilla." Brynne stood and pulled her sister's rigid body into her arms. Cilla resisted for a moment and then let Brynne hold her. After a minute, Brynne pulled away and led Cilla to the sofa with her. She patted the seat beside her and waited until Cilla took a seat before continuing.

"First of all, I'd gladly blow up half this cursed town if it would save Lucy's life. But it wouldn't, and you know that. Bethany Ridge was different. It's a tiny town in the middle of the Californian wilderness. We were basically on our own out there, so blowing up a few buildings and disrupting a hanging or two was a little more feasible out there. But this is Charlotte. It's a big city with a lot of people living in it. Staging a prison break would be a little more difficult to achieve out here."

"But not impossible," Cilla insisted.

Brynne looked thoughtful and a sliver of unease wormed its way into the ball of misery that used to be Finn's heart.

"No," she finally said. "Not impossible. We'd just have to be more careful about it."

"Wait," Finn said. "You two aren't seriously proposing we break Lucy out of jail."

Two sets of chocolate-brown eyes gazed at him.

"It'll never work, and then she'll be in even more trouble than she is now. Running only makes her look guilty."

Cilla snorted. "If you're too much of a coward to help my sister, then you can leave."

"My courage isn't what's in question here. It's your judgment. Brynne is right, even if we could get Lucy out of there, hiding her away forever would be next to impossible."

Cilla rolled her eyes. "You were raised by natives and have been working with smugglers for years. I'd be willing to bet the whole gold mine that you'd be very capable of taking Lucy and disappearing."

"Yes. I could. But is that what you really want? Is it what she'll want?"

"She wants to live."

"What kind of living would that be? You'd never see her again. We'd have to disappear and never return. Preferably to a foreign country where the government here couldn't touch her. Is that what you want for her? Because I guarantee you that's not what she wants for herself."

"At least she'd be free."

"Free to do what? Be on the run for the rest of her life? She could never have children. What kind of life would that be for them? She'd never see her family again, her home, the people and things she loves. What kind of a life is that?"

Cilla fumed, but she before she could speak again, Brynne cut in. "He's right."

"What?" Cilla asked, her face flaming red.

"He's right, Cilla. And you know it. Lucy wouldn't want to live like that."

"At least she'd live!"

Finn flinched at her words, but he didn't say anything, waiting silently with Brynne until Cilla calmed down. The fight had gone out of her with those last words. She knew what she was proposing was futile. If Finn thought for a moment it would work, he'd already be breaking down the jailhouse doors.

"We still have time," Brynne said quietly. "Richard and Leo are still out searching. And a jury might realize that Lucy is telling the truth and is innocent. She hasn't been convicted of anything just yet."

Finn nodded, fiery determination burning in his gut. "But if she is," he said, meeting Cilla's gaze, "then we'll talk."

Cilla nodded and gave him a slow smile.

Finally, they agreed on something.

• • •

The next time the cell door opened, Finn entered alone. Lucy took him in, her gaze hungrily raking over every inch of him. He stood at the door to the cell for a moment and just looked at her. Then he opened his arms and Lucy rushed to him, burying her face in his chest and breathing him in as he enveloped her in his embrace.

Every time she saw him she wondered if it would be the last. Would he decide that standing by her side was too much trouble? Too dangerous for him? And what if she was convicted? She didn't want him wasting his life waiting for her. Or worse yet, watching while she was executed.

"Come here," Finn said, drawing her to the narrow bunk against the wall.

He sat down, pulling her onto his lap. She curled against him, taking comfort from the steady beating of his heart. He ran his hand up and down her back.

"How are you doing?" he asked.

Lucy considered lying, telling him she was fine. He probably wouldn't believe her though.

"And don't tell me you're fine," he added.

Lucy laughed. "No, I'm not fine. I'm angry and uncomfortable and worried about the trial. But I am happy to see you."

Finn kissed the top of her head. "I tried to bribe the sheriff into letting me move in but he didn't bite."

Lucy snuggled closer. "Maybe we just need to offer him more money."

"It's worth a try." He kissed her forehead. "Though this bed is far too narrow." His lips brushed her cheek. "We'd definitely need something larger."

"Definitely," Lucy murmured, lifting her face to meet his lips.

Finn crushed her to him and Lucy wrapped her arms around his neck, starving for his touch.

"Hey!" a guard shouted.

Lucy jumped, but Finn kept her firmly planted on his lap.

"None of that, you hear? Or you'll be out of there right quick."

Finn glared at the officer but Lucy nodded. The guards had treated her fairly well for the most part and the last thing Lucy wanted was to lose any privileges, like being allowed visitors well past regular hours.

She gently extricated herself from Finn's arms, though

doing so felt like she was amputating part of herself, and sat beside him on the cot.

She shushed his growl of protest. "Hush. There'll be plenty of time for all that when I'm out of here."

Finn's lips tightened and Lucy's stomach dropped. She'd known he hadn't had good news when he'd walked through her cell door. Still, she'd hoped she was wrong. "What is it?" she asked. "You can't find her, can you?"

Finn shook his head and got up. He paced the cell, his long stride eating up the small space in two steps. "We've looked everywhere. Asked at the train stations, at every establishment within twenty miles of here. Richard and Leo are still searching with a team of men we've hired, combing every roadside shelter in every direction she might have gone. No one has seen her."

"Well," Lucy said, looking down at her hands. She tried to force as much cheerful optimism into her voice as she could, though she was far from feeling any. "I told her to disappear. Can hardly blame her for obeying me." She gave him a weak smile.

"Yes, I can. You are very likely going to be convicted of a murder you didn't commit and while I'm grateful to her for saving your life that day, it's doing you little good now if you are going to hang for it!"

Lucy stood and went to him, placing her palms on his chest to stop his pacing. She looked up into the face she adored, into the eyes that she saw every time she closed her own. "I can't fault her for trying to save her own life. I still have a chance. A good one, I think. I'm innocent and there is no evidence to suggest that I'm not."

Finn cupped her face in his hands. "They don't need evidence, Lucy. A pillar of their community was killed and they want blood for it. Anyone's blood. They don't care whose it is. They don't care if you are innocent or not. There is no one else to blame, and so they'll blame you. And I'll lose you."

His voice cracked and he swallowed hard and drew her nearer.

"We don't know what will happen," she insisted, reaching up to cover his hands with her own. "And for now we still have each other. We haven't lost each other yet."

"It's not enough." He leaned down and kissed her. "An eternity wouldn't be enough."

Lucy kissed him, molding herself as tightly to him as she could. He was right. She could have a lifetime of days and nights with him and would still ache for more.

"Come on," she said, drawing him back to the cot. "Talk to me."

Finn's eyebrows rose. "About what?" He settled down beside her, keeping her hands in his.

"Anything. What are we going to do once I'm out of here? Where will we go?"

"Lucy…"

"You asked me to run away with you not too long ago. Where were you going to take me?"

Finn's thumb rubbed over her knuckles, back and forth. "I thought we could go back to California, so you could be near your family."

"To the ranch?"

Finn nodded and gave her a faint smile. "I've never seen it. But Jake told me about it, in his letters. He loved it there." Finn laughed. "I thought perhaps your sister was a witch who'd bespelled him because never in all my born days would I have believed that Jacob Forrester would want to settle down with a girl and raise babies."

Lucy smiled. "Well, we Richardsons can be a formidable bunch. Once Brynne had decided she wanted him, he hardly stood a chance."

"That's true enough. A stubborn lot, all three of you."

Lucy looked at their entwined hands, her heart skipping with each soft brush of his fingers over hers. "It's strange to think that you were so close to me, but we didn't meet. Of course, had you met me then you would have run for the hills as fast as your feet could carry you."

"Love, I've been trying to make a run for it since the moment I clapped eyes on you."

Lucy gasped in mock outrage and slapped at him, but he smiled and pulled her back into his arms. "But no matter how hard I tried to stay away, something in those big brown eyes of yours keeps pulling me back."

"Well, I'm grateful for that at least. But when I get out of here I'm going to invest in a strong pair of chains to keep you from ever running again."

"I'll wear them gladly if they will keep you shackled to me. You get into entirely too much trouble when you are left to run amuck on your own."

"That sounds heavenly to me."

The guard came bustling back in and opened the cell door. "Time is up."

Finn stood, drawing Lucy up with him. Lucy clung to him, panic clawing at her. She was suddenly terrified that if he walked out that door, she'd never see him again.

He pulled her into a bone-crushing embrace, kissing her until her head spun. He pulled away just far enough so he could whisper in her ear. "The fight isn't over yet. Lilah or no Lilah, I will *not* let you hang."

He kissed her one last time and strode out the door, a new purpose in his step. Lucy watched him go with hope and terror warring in her heart.

For now, at least, the hope won, and for the first time in many days, she was able to sleep.

Chapter Eighteen

Finn watched as the woman darted across the street, holding her cloak tight about her against the cold night air. He waited until she came to the door of the dilapidated building where she'd been living, and then he stepped from the shadows.

"Lilah."

She gave a muffled shriek and clapped her hands over her mouth. "Mr. Finn, that you?"

"Yes. I'm sorry I frightened you."

Lilah rocked on her feet, her eyes darting around.

He held up a hand like he was trying to calm a skittish horse. "I'm alone. I just want to talk to you."

Lilah studied him and then nodded. She led him inside and he waited until she'd lit a lone candle and waved him into a chair by her cold hearth before he said anything.

He didn't waste any time but came right to the point. "She's going to hang."

Lilah blanched, her face puckering in distress. "I gotta come back. I can't let her hang, not for me. I'll come back. I'll tell them I done it."

"It's not quite that simple," Finn said, leaning forward to rest his elbows on his knees. "If the judge even allowed you to testify, none of us want to see you hang in Lucy's place, and she'd skin me alive if I allowed it."

Lilah shook her head, tears flowing down her face. "That Miz Lucy has the kindest heart I ever come across and that's the God's honest truth, but she the craziest woman I ever come across, too."

Finn snorted. "No argument here."

"So, what can we do?"

"We need to show Halford for who he really is. There's no denying you killed him, but you killed an evil man to save two innocent lives. There's no crime in that. We just need to prove it. And I need your help."

"I'll do anything I can."

Finn nodded. "Good. Now, I've been Halford's right-hand man for long enough that I know where to find certain incriminating documents and possibly some stores of contraband that the authorities won't be able to ignore. As long as I can get to them and he hasn't moved them."

"And what do you need me to do?"

"A lot of the evidence I need is at Philip's house and I can't get near it at the moment. Even though Halford is dead, his servants still see me as an extension of him. They won't speak to me. I need you to get me inside, get the servants to talk to me, convince them to give statements. The more evidence we have against him, the better."

Lilah nodded. "I can do that. But I gotta own up to what I done, too. I can't let no innocent woman, especially someone like Miz Lucy, suffer any more for what I done."

Finn hesitated.

"Mr. Finn, you know it's the only way to make sure she don't hang."

Finally, he nodded. Lilah was a good woman and she'd

saved his life, and Lucy's. For that, he'd owe her a lifetime. But Lucy could *not* hang. And Lilah was right. It was the only way to be sure she wouldn't.

"Lucy will be furious, at both of us, though me especially, I think. But, we won't abandon you. Lucy's lawyer will defend you. I promise you, you won't hang."

Lilah shook her head. "You can't promise me that. It don't matter though. I can't let Miz Lucy hang."

Finn took Lilah's hand. "I can promise it. If they do convict you, I'll break into the prison myself and get you out. You will *not* hang. But Lucy will if we don't do something."

Lilah stood. "Then we'd better hurry."

Finn released a long breath. "We had indeed."

• • •

Lucy thought often of that restful night of sleep over the next several days. It was the last peace she had. The last opportunity she'd had to see Finn. Her trial had begun. The case was so notorious the city wanted it over and done with as soon as possible. Those who'd supported Philip called out for justice to be served. Those who knew Lucy called out for her acquittal.

Unfortunately, Lucy had former slaves and poor white laborers on her side, while Philip had some of the most influential people in North Carolina, and beyond, on his. No one would listen to those who spoke of Lucy's kindness and generosity. The papers painted her as a loose woman of questionable morals who'd tried to trap the virtuous Philip and when that hadn't worked, she'd killed him in a fit of jealousy.

Her injuries at the time she was taken were chalked up to a fight with another lover, a mysterious savage who'd been shot and killed by Philip when he'd found the man and his ladylove in flagrante delicto. No one seemed to connect Finn, who'd continued to hide his tattoos, to the tattooed mystery man, nor did they find it strange that Philip's right-hand man was Lucy's staunchest supporter. Or if they did, they ignored it in the interest of a juicier tale. No one seemed interested in the truth. Least of all the jury of her so-called peers.

Mr. Fitzhugh had few defense witnesses he could call, nearly all of them serving only as character witnesses who testified to Lucy's kindness, generosity, and general sweet disposition. Unfortunately, all but two of the witnesses were the lower-class whites and former slaves whose testimonies the jury didn't even pretend to listen to. No matter what laws had been passed after the Civil War, laws Mr. Fitzhugh insisted the court follow, folks still weren't keen on seeing blacks in the courtroom. Though Lucy's friends were testifying for her and not necessarily against Mr. Halford, it was obvious their presence was unwanted and having them there at all showed how desperate Mr. Fitzhugh was to find someone to speak well of Lucy.

Lucy and Mr. Fitzhugh had gone back and forth on whether or not she should take the stand in her own defense. Mr. Fitzhugh didn't want to give the prosecution any more ammunition than they already had, should Lucy answer a question in an unflattering way. But Lucy was hopeful if they could just hear her side of the story from her own lips, that she'd be able to sway enough of them.

Mr. Fitzhugh leaned over to whisper in Lucy's ear. "There is one more witness I can call. I know you will object, but—"

Lucy was already shaking her head. "No. You will not call Finn."

"He has evidence to submit that will prove what kind of man Halford is. It might help your case. It's the only card we've got left."

"No," Lucy insisted. "He can't present that evidence

without incriminating himself. It won't do me any good to be acquitted just to see the man I love hang for crimes he was compelled to commit. Leave Finn out of this."

"Miss Richardson…"

"I said no. If you attempt to call Finn to the stand, I will fire you on the spot and defend myself."

Mr. Fitzhugh gave her a withering look but nodded in agreement.

"Call me to the stand."

He sighed and stood. "Your honor, I call Miss Lucy Richardson to the stand."

Lucy glanced back to see Finn, his face red with fury. He half stood and Lucy shook her head, pleading with him to understand, trying to put all the love she felt for him in her eyes.

She walked slowly to her seat, her head held high, though her insides were quivering like Brynne's Christmas pudding. She placed her hand on the Bible held before her and proclaimed in a loud clear voice that she would say nothing but the truth, so help her God.

And then the questions began.

Mr. Fitzhugh led her through the events of the day, and she told her story minus a few of the more scandalous details that she hoped wouldn't need to be revealed. The prosecutor, Mr. Button, apparently had other ideas.

"Miz Richardson, isn't it true that when you came to our fair city, you registered at the Chatford Hotel as Miz Lucy Taggart?"

Lucy hesitated, but she had to answer. "Well, yes, but—"

"And isn't it true that you knowingly lied to Mr. Philip Halford about who you were and what your purpose in coming to Charlotte was?"

"No, I—"

"So you informed Mr. Halford as to your true identity?"

"No, but…"

"What was your purpose in coming to Charlotte?"

"I came looking for a friend."

"I see. And what would that friend's name be?"

Lucy's stomach flipped. She didn't want to drag Finn into this.

"Miz Richardson?"

"Finnegan Taggart."

"Is this the same Finnegan Taggart who was employed by the deceased and who you identified as your cousin?"

"Well, no. Mr. Taggart was employed by Mr. Halford, but I never told him Mr. Taggart was my cousin. Someone else did."

"But you didn't correct the misunderstanding, did you?"

"No."

"And since you continued to use the name in the community, it is reasonable to conclude that Mr. Halford remained under the impression that you were in fact Mr. Taggart's cousin until the day of his death."

"Objection, Your Honor," Mr. Fitzhugh said. "My client has no way of knowing what Mr. Halford did or did not think."

"Sustained," the judge said. But he didn't look happy about it.

Mr. Button nodded and pursed his lips. "Miz Richardson, did you ever refer to Mr. Taggart as your cousin in Mr. Halford's hearing?"

Lucy's stomach dropped lower. "Yes."

"Did Mr. Halford ever refer to Mr. Taggart as your cousin in your hearing?"

"Yes."

"So you presented yourself to Mr. Halford as a cousin of his trusted employee. To what purpose?"

"Objection, Your Honor," Mr. Fitzhugh broke in again. "None of this is relevant to the case."

"The relevance will be made known, Your Honor, if you'll allow me a little leeway," Button said.

The judge nodded. "Overruled."

Mr. Fitzhugh sat back down, his jaw clenched tight. Lucy kept her back straight, hoping an outward appearance of calm would hide the chaos of emotions bubbling beneath the surface.

"Answer the question please."

"I didn't have any purpose really for saying Mr. Taggart was my cousin. It was just easier to not correct the assumption."

"So, because it was easier than telling the truth, you allowed Mr. Halford to believe, throughout the course of his courtship of you, that you were the cousin of Mr. Taggart."

"I…we didn't really have a courtship."

"Relevance, Your Honor!" Mr. Fitzhugh shouted from his table.

Mr. Button held up his hand, his chest puffing up to twice its size. He turned a predatory gaze on Lucy, who had to pinch her thigh to keep from flinching.

"The relevance is that Mr. Halford entered into a courtship with a woman he believed to be the close kinswoman of a trusted friend and employee, a woman who has just admitted that she knowingly lied to Mr. Halford about her identity so that she could seduce him for her own as yet undiscovered, nefarious purposes. Believing her lies as he did, when he found them, in Miz Richardson's bedchamber, entwined together as only a man and wife should be, the shock of it all sent poor Mr. Halford into such a state that he reacted as any man in love would. And when this deceitful, disgraceful woman thought her lover was being threatened, she attacked Mr. Halford, striking him over the head with such force that she bashed his brains in. Isn't that true, Miz Richardson?"

There was a collective gasp from the audience and Lucy's gaze darted around frantically, trying to find someone, anyone, who might still be looking at her with sympathy.

"No...no..."

Only...it was true. It had happened exactly as Mr. Button had said. Without adding the facts about Philip's true nature, his ties to the smuggling ring, the KKK, his forced indenture of Finn, Philip did seem like an unwitting victim. And there was no way to prove he was anything else. Or that Lucy was anything other than a lying, deceitful murderess.

"Your honor!" Finn stood, leaning over the partition that separated the audience from the court participants.

"Order!" the judge said.

"Your honor, I have evidence to present that will prove that Mr. Halford was not the upstanding citizen he presented himself as."

The courtroom was in an uproar. Mr. Button shouted that Finn had no right to speak, Mr. Fitzhugh yelled at Mr. Button, the audience members were beside themselves with the drama, and Lucy's sisters were shouting themselves hoarse that Finn should be heard.

"Enough! Order! Order!" the judge yelled, banging his gavel with such vehemence Lucy thought it would go straight through the desk.

"Bailiff! Remove that man from my court, at once!"

Lucy covered her mouth to keep from crying out. Finn kept shouting, listing all Philip's crimes as he was dragged from the courtroom. No one paid any attention to him. And no one cared about anything else Lucy or her lawyer had to say.

Mr. Button rested. Mr. Fitzhugh had no choice but to rest as well.

It took the jury only twenty-three minutes to find her guilty.

Chapter Nineteen

Lucy had to wait for her formal sentencing. Alone, in her cell. They wouldn't let her see anyone but her lawyer, and he had precious little hope to share with her. They both knew she'd hang.

Lucy knew she should be terrified, but all she felt was a sad sort of calm. It was over. No more anticipation, no more false hope, no more wondering and praying. Just resignation.

As long as she didn't think about Finn.

The thought of leaving him behind shredded the last remaining thread of soul she had left. She was sad to be leaving her sisters as well. Regretted that she wouldn't get to see her nieces and nephews grow up.

But Finn...he was what made her want to curl up in a ball of misery and howl at the fates that had led her to this moment. She wasn't proud of the thoughts that ran through her head, but in her weakest moments she cursed Lilah and herself and even God for giving Finn back to her only to rip her away from him again. Only this time it would be permanent. What sort of cruel deity would toy with them like this? Let them spend one glorious day in each other's arms only to lose each other forever?

But thoughts like those brought her to the brink of despair, and she couldn't afford to fall over that ledge. She had an execution to get through. And she would go to it with her head held high. She was innocent, and she wouldn't let her enemies make her cower.

And so she prayed. She spent hours on her knees, praying for forgiveness, for strength, for courage. She didn't sleep much. She didn't want to waste the last moments of her life oblivious to the world, though it was tempting to slip into her dreams. In her dreams, she was with Finn again, married, watching their children play, growing old together. They were wonderful, beautiful dreams. But waking from them was a cruel torture that she dreaded more with each night.

On the third day, Lucy heard her prison door open and looked up to see Finn walking in. She sprang at him, launching herself into his arms before she'd even realized she'd moved.

Finn gathered her close and held her, wiping away the tears she hadn't realized were running down her cheeks.

"How did you get them to let you in?"

"A big fat bribe," Finn said with a smile that quickly melted away. "I've been trying to get in since the trial. But they wouldn't let me come until now."

"I'm glad you're here." Lucy wrapped her arms around him and buried her face in his neck.

"Lucy, I'm sorry, so sorry for all those years I wasted. I should have come back. I should never have left at all. When I think—"

"Shhh," Lucy said, stroking her hands through his hair. She kissed him, long and hard, and when she pulled away, it was to find his tears mingling with hers.

She pulled him close again, pressed her cheek to his so she could whisper in his ear. "This…this is what I'll be thinking of.

How your arms feel wrapped so tightly around me. What your hands feel like on my skin. The sound of your heart beating with mine. This. This moment. This is what will give me the strength I need."

"Lucy." Her name was a choked whisper on his lips. Finn brushed her hair from her face, his thumbs stroking her cheeks. He leaned down and kissed her, his lips drinking her in with a desperation that consumed them both.

"I love you," he murmured, kissing her again and again. "I've loved you since the moment you walked into my life. I've wasted so much time when I should have been telling you every day how much you mean to me."

"Hush, my love. I've always known. Even when you refused to admit it."

"I guess you aren't the only one who can be stubborn."

Lucy's laugh mingled with a sob. "Heaven forbid."

Finn crushed her to him. "I'm not going to let them do this. Your sisters and I are coming up with a plan. We'll get you out of this."

Fresh fear spiked through Lucy and she grabbed Finn's face, forced him to look at her. "No, Finn."

He opened his mouth to argue, but Lucy cut him off. "No. The only way I can bear this is if I know the rest of you will go on living, if I can picture you happy, having a long, full life. I want you to leave here, before it happens. Make my sisters go. I don't want any of you to see...to see..."

Lucy stopped, unable to force the words from her mouth. "Lucy..."

She shook her head, wanting to finish what she had to say. "Mr. Fitzhugh helped me draw up a will. I'm leaving you my share of the mine and the ranch in California. If you don't want to stay there, let my sisters buy you out. Use your share of the mine profits and find a place somewhere you can be happy."

"I can't be happy without you!"

"You will. In time."

Finn stepped away from her, breathing as though he'd just run ten miles. He shook his head and grabbed her arms, hauling her back to him. "No." He tucked her head under his chin, held her so tightly she could barely breathe. But she wouldn't have moved for anything in the world.

"No," he repeated again. He kissed her forehead. "No." Kissed her eyes, her cheeks. "No."

Finally, he kissed her lips once more. "There is no happiness for me without you. Ever."

His lips covered hers, his mouth ravishing her, branding her as his.

The cell door opened once more and someone cleared his throat. Finn ignored it. But Lucy gently pulled away.

Mr. Fitzhugh waited with an officer to escort her to the courtroom.

Lucy gazed back at Finn, gave him a sad smile and stroked his cheek. "They can't take anything from me," she said quietly. "You are my life."

She pressed one last kiss to his lips. "I love you," she whispered.

She walked away, leaving him standing alone in the middle of the cell.

Lucy sat beside Mr. Fitzhugh as the jury filed in. Stood as the judge entered. Sat when told. Heard nothing but vague mutterings as the judge spoke. Her world had narrowed to the man she'd left in the jail cell. The man who was sitting beside her sisters in the observation balcony.

Nothing else mattered to her. Nothing else penetrated the haze surrounding her.

Mr. Fitzhugh touched her elbow, helping her to stand when the jury foreman stood to read her sentence.

She didn't look at him. She turned so she could meet Finn's gaze. Replayed the last moments they'd had together over and over.

"We the jury…"

I love you.

"Sentence the accused, Miss Lucy Richardson…"

I've loved you since the moment you walked into my life.

"To hang by the neck until dead."

You are my life.

"And may God have mercy on your soul."

Lucy closed her eyes, letting her tears fall, shutting out everything, everyone.

"No!"

Lucy's eyes flew open and she looked around the courtroom. She knew that voice. The judge banged his gavel, trying to silence the sudden uproar.

"She didn't do it! She's innocent. You can't hang her."

"Lilah?" Lucy said, finally locating the woman in the back of the courtroom.

Lilah had rushed into the aisle, but a bailiff had stopped her. She tried to push him off, but he held tight.

"Bring her here," the judge ordered.

Lucy looked up at Finn who was now nearly hanging over the balcony. His startled gaze met hers. But what made Lucy's heart pound was the look on his face. There was hope in his eyes again. Her sisters beside him were pale and clinging to one another for support, but they too had lost the look of despair they'd both worn for the last several weeks.

Mr. Fitzhugh patted her on the shoulder and Lucy slumped back into her chair, her hand over her mouth.

The bailiff brought Lilah before the judge.

"What's your name?" he ordered.

"Lilah, sir."

"What was your mas— What's your surname?"

"Lilah Halford, sir."

There was a collective gasp in the courtroom. Even the judge's brows rose a bit.

"And why did you feel the need to burst into my courtroom? Miss Richardson has already been tried and convicted of Mr. Halford's murder."

"But she didn't do it! I did."

Lucy's hands trembled and she gripped them together in her lap. There were so many emotions rushing through her she wasn't sure which to focus on. Hope for herself, fear for Lilah, anxiety for Finn who was still hanging precariously close to the edge of the balcony and looked as though he were ready to jump over to have his say so at any moment.

The judge spoke again. "Then why are you just coming forward now? This seems to me nothing more than a delay tactic, a scheme to try and save her from the noose where she rightfully belongs. I'll not have such hysterics in my courtroom. Bailiff!"

The officer grasped Lilah again and made to haul her off, but Lilah pulled from his grasp.

"I can prove I done it!"

She swung the burlap bag she'd been clutching in her hand and slammed it onto the judge's desk.

"What is this? What do you think you're doing?"

"It's a fry pan, sir. It's what I kilt Mr. Halford with."

Another gasp broke out and the judge banged his gavel again. Once some semblance of order had returned, the judge sat for a moment, clearly at a loss as how to proceed. Finally, he nodded and the bailiff came forward, pulled a handkerchief from his pocket, and gingerly opened the bag. He extracted the heavy iron pan, still crusted with Philip's blood, and dropped it back on the table.

Mr. Button stood up. "Your Honor, I must object. This woman worked for Miss Richardson. She'd probably say anything to keep her from hanging. She could have picked up the frying pan and scurried it away at some point, to be used if the tides turned against them."

There were murmurs of agreement from the audience and the judge banged his gavel again.

"I'm of a mind to agree with you, Mr. Button, but as the woman just plunked a bloody pan down on my desk I'm at least curious enough to hear her out."

Lucy released a breath she hadn't noticed she'd been holding.

Lilah was led to the witness chair and Lucy could see her trembling. She leaned over to Mr. Fitzhugh.

"Help her, please. I'll retain you for your services. She needs counsel."

Mr. Fitzhugh nodded and stood. "Your Honor, I've just been retained as counsel for Miss Halford. May I have a quick word with her?"

The judge frowned but nodded. "A very quick word. This is all irregular enough. I'd like to get this circus over with sooner rather than later."

Mr. Fitzhugh nodded and went to Lilah. After a few moments of hurried whispers, he came back to their table. "Miss Halford would like to formally confess to the murder of Mr. Philip Halford."

"And what proof do you have?" Mr. Button insisted.

"Aside from that bloody pan," Lilah said, skewering the attorney with a glare, "I can tell you details that nobody that weren't there would know."

"Such as?" Mr. Button asked.

Lucy leaned over the Mr. Fitzhugh. "You can't let her confess. Then *she'll* be hanged."

Mr. Fitzhugh whispered back. "She's insisting. Nothing I

said would dissuade her."

Lucy sat back and glanced up at Finn. He looked worried but gave her an encouraging smile.

Lilah went through the details of the moments leading up to the murder. She described the scene perfectly. Described where Philip was standing, what had happened, what he'd said. How she'd come in and heard Philip threatening Lucy and Finn. When she heard the gunshot she grabbed the frying pan and snuck up behind him.

"I'd thought I'd only scare him, knock him cold maybe. I never intended to hurt him so bad. But if I hadn't done it, he'd have kilt Mr. Taggart for sure, and maybe done worse to Miz Lucy. His men had already hurt her bad enough, as anyone could see who saw her that day. I did what I had to do to save Miz Lucy and Mr. Taggart."

The judge called for the lead officer who'd been there that day to step forward. "Does Miss Halford's description of the events measure up to what you saw that day?"

The pasty-faced officer looked like he was sucking a lemon as he answered, but he nodded his head. "Yes, she described it accurately."

"They could have collaborated on a story, made sure their tales would match up," Mr. Button insisted.

The officer shook his head. "There were witnesses on the scene almost immediately. When we arrived, Miss Richardson was still on the floor trying to stop Mr. Taggart's bleeding. There wouldn't have been time to discuss a story, and Miss Richardson has been in custody since then."

The judge sat back, looking back and forth between Lucy and Lilah. Then finally, he sat forward and said, "I'm inclined to agree. Mr. Button?"

Mr. Button, his face mottled red, stood and glared at Lucy. But he said, "In light of this new evidence, the prosecution has no objection to all charges being dropped against Miss

Richardson."

"Agreed," the judge said and banged his gavel. "Miss Lucy Richardson, you are hereby acquitted of the murder of Mr. Philip Halford."

Lucy covered her hands with her mouth, unable to keep back the gasp of joy that leaped inside her. Chaos broke out in the courtroom. The judge banged his gavel until it broke. Then he chucked the pieces over his shoulder, got up from his bench and left.

Lucy's joy was short-lived. In the ensuing chaos, no one else noticed as the bailiff grasped Lilah's arm and led her from the courtroom. Before she was taken through the doors, she stopped and met Lucy's gaze. Lucy looked at her friend, her eyes swimming with unshed tears. Lilah gave her a sad smile and let the bailiff lead her away.

Chapter Twenty

Lucy stretched, carefully extricating her arm from beneath Finn. He stirred but didn't waken and Lucy curled on her side and watched him sleep. With the lines of his face softened by sleep, he looked years younger. Almost like the young man she'd first met so many years ago. She reached out a gentle finger and brushed a lock of hair off his forehead, overwhelmed with happiness at the thought that she'd get to wake up to his beloved face every day for the rest of her life.

After Lucy had been released, Finn had taken her straight to the first judge he could track down and demanded that they be married immediately. Lucy had no objection. And though her sisters had been a bit disappointed that they didn't get to throw her a huge church wedding, everyone had been so euphoric over the outcome of Lilah's revelation, no one had voiced any real complaints.

Lucy frowned. Lilah was the one concern that marred her happiness. Mr. Fitzhugh was very optimistic, more so than he'd been for Lucy, which, all things considered, was something indeed.

"What has put such a frown on your face?" Finn asked, his sleepy voice breaking into her thoughts. "I know it couldn't be anything I've done...or didn't do," he said with a wicked smile.

Lucy's stomach flipped at the reminder of how they'd spent their hours the night before. Just the memory made her toes tingle.

Finn drew a lazy finger across her brow, smoothing out the crease, and continued trailing it down her face until he reached her lips.

Lucy kissed his fingertip and then nuzzled her face in his hand.

"What's wrong, love?" he asked.

"I'm just worried about Lilah."

Finn pulled Lucy down for a kiss and then tucked her against him. "I'm actually very hopeful. Mr. Fitzhugh has been beside himself at the evidence we were able to give him. Coming from Lilah, they can be presented without implicating me, which fulfills your requirement that I keep out of it," he said, pulling her closer. "Things are looking very good for her indeed."

"I hope so," Lucy said. "You never told me what sort of evidence you turned over."

"You didn't want to hear about it at the time," Finn gently reminded her.

"Well my plate was a bit full at the moment."

Finn laughed. "Very true. Well, once I found Lilah, I was able to get back onto Halford's property. More importantly, with Lilah's help, I was able to get the servants to trust me enough to cooperate with me. After Halford's death, they'd begun cleaning out the house, putting everything in storage, which made finding the evidence I needed very difficult. But with Lilah to smooth the way, we were able to find what we needed.

"We went back to the shacks on Halford's property."

"The shacks?" Lucy shivered. "But what about…those men, what happened to…?"

"Lilah and I buried them."

Lucy's eyes widened and Finn continued. "They won't be found, and I doubt anyone misses them. If any of the servants saw what we did, they won't betray us."

Lucy let that sink in for a moment and then nodded. "What did you find when you went back?"

"With the help of Halford's staff, who were only too happy to assist now that Halford was no longer there to beat terror into them, we recovered the secret shipments he'd been ferrying in. Cases of opium had been stockpiled, and the crates of contraband. I was also able to retrieve the papers and ledgers and it all proved how corrupt Halford was."

"Well, glad to discover you kept busy while I was locked up," Lucy said with an attempt at levity. In truth, she was overwhelmed with what her husband and her friend had gone through in order to set her free.

"Lilah did society a favor by getting rid of Halford, and I think there are very few people left who don't agree. Add to the fact that Halford was the only one armed in the whole altercation and had already shot me and was threatening to harm you, Mr. Fitzhugh says that Lilah's act is being hailed by many as heroic. She might be given a cursory sentence since she had, in fact, killed the man, but the main consensus seems to be that the verdict will be light."

"I hope so, but I won't rest easy until Lilah is free."

"I know, my love. And we'll do everything we can to ensure she is."

Lucy buried her head against Finn's chest and breathed deeply.

With a sudden growl, Finn rolled, pulling Lucy along with him. She yelped in surprise, giggling as Finn rolled her beneath him.

"There's only one sure way I know to keep your mind off your troubles," he said. He ground his hips against her and Lucy gasped, arching into him. All thoughts of anything but the magnificent man above her evaporated on a wave of love and desire, and Finn gamely kept her distracted until they fell back into a satisfyingly exhausted sleep.

Epilogue

Lucy stepped down from the coach and took a deep breath, filling her lungs with the clean, Californian air. She was home. She had never seen anything so beautiful. The house nestled in its clearing. The stables and paddocks spread out behind the house, flowing into the cow pastures. The ranch's garden was bursting with vegetables, and Lucy's mouth was already watering at the thought of sinking her teeth into one of the crisp apples from the orchard. She felt like she'd died and gone to heaven.

A squeal from the direction of the house stole her attention and she braced herself as Carmen, the Richardson's housekeeper and surrogate mother, came barreling out of the house. She crashed into Lucy and swept her into a smothering hug.

"Ah, *mija*, you're home at last," Carmen said, backing away just enough to squish Lucy's cheeks between her hands.

Lucy laughed and returned Carmen's hug. "It's long overdue, I know."

Miguel, Carmen's husband, hung back, waiting for his

wife to finish her hellos before he came to envelope Lucy in his arms. "It's good to have you home. We'll have to make sure we keep you here this time, eh?"

"I think we'll be sticking around awhile," Lucy said, glancing back at the coach where Finn was unloading their luggage.

"So," Carmen said, her hands on her hips as she sized up Finn, "you are the one who stole our Lucy's heart."

"And brought me home," Lucy reminded her.

"For that," Carmen said, opening her arms wide to give him a welcoming hug, "we'll be forever grateful. Welcome home."

Finn nodded, his eyes looking suspiciously bright to Lucy. But he went back to the luggage and the moment was lost in a flurry of activity as Cilla and Leo and their son clambered down and came forward for their hugs and kisses.

It wasn't until later that night, when Finn and Lucy were settled in the bunkhouse, where they'd stay until their own home could be built on the property, that Lucy had a chance to gauge how Finn was really feeling.

"Are you happy we decided to move out here?" she asked.

Finn smiled and pulled her into his arms. "Of course, I am. Why do you ask?"

Lucy shrugged. "I don't know. You've just been quiet tonight."

Finn burrowed them down farther in the pillows. "It's a lot to take in. I'm used to being on my own. Not…"

"Not part of such a loud, obnoxious family?"

Finn laughed. "Your words, my dear."

Lucy smiled but pressed on, wanting to make sure of his feelings. "Will you be happy here?"

Finn tilted her face to his, pressed a tender kiss to her lips. "I will be happy anywhere you are, love. And this place…in this place…I can be myself. It's been a very long time since

I've had a place I could call home."

Lucy drew her finger along the tattoos on his chin; let her thumb trail along the T-shaped marks on his cheeks. She'd wiped the makeup from his handsome face the moment they'd entered the bunkhouse. And she didn't want to ever see them covered again. They were part of who he was—her wonderful, miraculous husband.

She leaned up to kiss him, her heart so full of love and happiness she felt she'd burst from it. Finn deepened the kiss, pressing her back against the feather mattress beneath them.

"I only need you," he murmured. "You are my home."

She gazed deep into his eyes and smiled. "And you are mine, my love."

• • •

Lucy stood on the platform, her eyes glued to the horizon. Brynne, Richard, and their children were due to arrive at any moment. It had been a year since Lucy had said good-bye to them and now, finally, they were coming to California for good.

After Lucy's ordeal, the ranch had become the haven they so desperately needed. Finn could be himself there, though it did take a little while for the townspeople to get used to him. But he was accepted there as he never would have been in Boston and certainly not in North Carolina. And most of his time was spent on the ranch. He had a good hand with horses and under his care, the horse stock on the ranch were flourishing.

Lucy had restarted the town school and had been very happy to discover how many adults in town were interested in attending the night classes she offered for them.

Cilla and Leo had always been at home on the ranch and had welcomed Lucy and Finn with open arms. Lucy and Finn had their own house on the property now, a beautiful home perfect for their new family. They were close enough to the main house that they could keep each other in view, but far enough away that they had their privacy.

And now Brynne and Richard were coming. The town was in need of a good doctor and Richard had insisted that he would be happy anywhere there were patients who needed him. And he knew Brynne would be happiest if she could be near her sisters.

The train blew its whistle in the distance and Lucy grasped her skirts, leaning over the edge of the platform to try and see around the bend. The excitement coursing through her had her nearly bouncing on her toes. Finally, they'd all be together again!

Finn laughingly came up behind her and wrapped his arms about her waist. "You'd best be careful, love, or you might fall right off the platform."

"Oh hush," Lucy said, playfully batting at his arm.

The train pulled around the bend and Lucy nearly jumped out of Finn's arms. "They're here!"

Finn laughed and let her go. Lucy waited eagerly as the train pulled in, its wheels squealing as they ground to a halt. The moment it stopped one of the passenger car doors burst open and Brynne tumbled out and into Lucy's arms. Richard followed with their children and shook Finn's hand. Then they stood and watched with loving smiles as their wives greeted one another.

They chattered over the top of one another until Richard held up a hand, pointing back to the train. A huge smile broke out on Brynne's face and she grabbed Lucy, spun her around, and clapped her hands over her eyes.

"What are you doing?" Lucy said, trying to pull Brynne's hands from her eyes.

"We have a surprise for you," Brynne said. "Are you

ready?"

Lucy laughed. "Yes!"

"All right. Open your eyes."

Brynne removed her hands and Lucy blinked a few times and looked in the direction Brynne had pointed her.

Lucy stared for a moment, struck dumb with shock. And then she clapped her hands over her mouth to muffle her shriek of joy. She ran forward and wrapped Lilah in a bear hug that nearly crushed the smaller woman. The two women sobbed as they clung together.

Finally, Lucy pulled away and clasped Lilah's face in her hands. "You're here. I'm speechless. I'm absolutely thrilled to see you, but what are you doing here?'"

Lilah looked down a little shyly. "Miz Oliver said there might be a place for me at the school here, or on the ranch. After…after everything that happened back there, well… there weren't nothin' there to stay for."

"Of course there is a place for you! I could use the help, surely. And there is always plenty of work to be done on the ranch as well. But what about…?"

Lilah smiled and turned around. Ruby, Sam, and their boys stood on the platform. Lucy went to them, hugging them each in turn and then went back to Lilah.

"I can never thank you enough for everything you've done for me," Lucy said, emotion choking her words. "I am so happy you are here."

"So am I, Miz Lucy. So am I."

The rest of the day was one of chaotic joy, getting everyone settled in, Brynne's family in the main house with Cilla, Lilah's family in the bunkhouse until a house could be built for them on the property.

After supper, when everyone had gone off to their various houses to turn in for the day, Lucy wandered out onto her porch and leaned against the railing. Finn joined her, standing beside her with an arm draped over her shoulders. Lucy leaned against him and sighed.

"What are you thinking?" he asked.

Lucy rubbed her face on his chest, staring out into the setting sun. "I don't think I've ever been so happy in all my days. It's a little overwhelming." She looked up at her husband with a smile. "But I hope it never ends."

Finn leaned down and kissed her. "We have each other. And the Richardson sisters are all together again. How could life be any more perfect?"

Lucy glanced up at him with a sly smile. "I can think of one thing…"

Finn laughed and scooped her up into his arms. "You read my mind, love."

He kissed her and carried her into their home, closing the door behind him.

Acknowledgments

To Erin Molta, Heidi Stryker, and Gwen Hayes—I am seriously the luckiest writer in the world to have you ladies. I can't tell you enough how much I appreciate all you do. Thank you a million times over.

To Babs Hightower—you are a writer's dream. Thank you so much for all the work you do to get my novels out in the world and in front of the people who will love them.

A huge thank-you to my sweet family for all their love and support. I promise someday the house will be clean and all your meals will be hot and on time. And in the meantime, I'll keep the cereal coming and…well, there's not much I can do about the house, but know that I love you more than anything in the world and am more grateful than I can say that you support me in this crazy business.

And to my readers, you guys are the reason I do what I do. Thank you so much for reading my stories.

About the Author

Romance and nonfiction author Michelle McLean is a jeans-and-T-shirt kind of girl who secretly wishes she could run around town in a big, poofy dress from the 1600s and hopes to someday be able to get away with crazy stuff like that by chalking it up to her eccentric writer personality. She's addicted to chocolate and Goldfish crackers and occasionally writes by hand just so she can hear the scratchy sound of her favorite gel pen on a sheet of paper. Her husband also swears she has conversations with herself, but she and the voices in her head, heartily disagree.

Michelle is a contributor to The Naked Hero, Operation Awesome, and Scene 13 blogs. You can find Michelle at her website, her blog, on Twitter, Facebook, Tumblr, and Pinterest.

In addition to her husband and two awesome kids, she also has two amazing stepkids and one beyond-adorable step-grandson. She currently resides in Pennsylvania with her husband and two kidlets, an insanely hyper dog, and two very spoiled cats.

Get Scandalous with these historical reads...

REAL EARLS BREAK THE RULES

an *Infamous Somertons* novel by Tina Gabrielle

Brandon St. Clair, the Earl of Vale, has never been one to follow the rules. Even though he must marry a wealthy heiress so that he can be rid of the pile of debt he inherited with his title, he can't stop thinking of another. Amelia Somerton is the daughter of a forger and is *not* a suitable wife. But that doesn't stop Brandon from making Amelia a different offer, the kind that breaks every rule of etiquette... But what begins as a simple arrangement, soon escalates into much more, and as the heat between them sizzles, each encounter becomes a lesson in seduction.

SEDUCING THE MARQUESS

a *Lords and Ladies in Love* novel by Callie Hutton

Richard, the Marquess of Devon is satisfied with his ton marriage. His wife of five months, Lady Eugenia Devon wants her very proper husband to fall in love with her. After finding a naughty book, she begins a campaign to change the rules. Her much changed and decidedly wicked behavior drives her husband to wonder if his perfect Lady has taken a lover. But the only man Eugenia wants is her husband. The book can bring sizzling desire to the marriage or cause an explosion.

TO WIN A VISCOUNT
a *Daughters of Amhurst* novel by Frances Fowlkes

To gain a certain marquess's notice, Lady Albina Beauchamp aims to win the derby and asks a handsome groom to train her. Although groom Edmund White believes beautiful Lady Albina's notions of racing are ridiculous, her determination, pluck, and spirit have him not only agreeing to help, but asking for payment: each lesson for a kiss.

THE EARL'S WAGER
a *Reluctant Bride* novel by Rebecca Thomas

When straight laced earl, Will Sutton, is challenged to turn an obstinate American ward, Miss Georgia Duvall, into a biddable lady suitable for the Marriage Mart, he gladly takes the wager. Then has to decide whether the prize--a prime racing stud horse--is worth changing the impudent beauty's temperament he's come to enjoy. Greatly.

CPSIA information can be obtained
at www.ICGtesting.com
Printed in the USA
LVHW101127030722
722671LV00019B/162

9 781943 892310